"I'm not going anywhere. I'm a man of my word."

She met his gaze. "Somehow I knew that."

"No matter how long it takes, I'm not leaving you." Austin knew even as he made the promise that there would be hell to pay with his family. She started to turn away.

"One more thing," he said. "Did your sister have a key to this house?"

"No." Realization dawned on her expression. She shivered.

"Then there is nothing to worry about," he said. "Try to get some sleep."

"You, too."

He knew that wouldn't be easy. An electricity seemed to spark in the air between them. They'd been through so much together already. He didn't dare imagine what tomorrow would bring.

DEC 1 4

DELIVERANCE AT CARDWELL RANCH

New York Times *Bestselling Author*

B.J. DANIELS

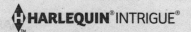

HARLEQUIN® INTRIGUE®

Recycling programs
for this product may
not exist in your area.

ISBN-13: 978-0-373-69800-4

Deliverance at Cardwell Ranch

Copyright © 2014 by Barbara Heinlein

This edition published by arrangement with Harlequin Books S.A.

For questions and comments about the quality of this book, please contact us at CustomerService@Harlequin.com.

Printed in U.S.A.

ABOUT THE AUTHOR

New York Times bestselling author B.J. Daniels wrote her first book after a career as an award-winning newspaper journalist and author of thirty-seven published short stories. That first book, *Odd Man Out*, received a four-and-a-half-star review from *RT Book Reviews* and went on to be nominated for Best Intrigue that year. Since then, she has won numerous awards, including a career achievement award for romantic suspense and many nominations and awards for best book.

Daniels lives in Montana with her husband, Parker, and two springer spaniels, Spot and Jem. When she isn't writing, she snowboards, camps, boats and plays tennis. Daniels is a member of Mystery Writers of America, Sisters in Crime, International Thriller Writers, Kiss of Death and Romance Writers of America.

To contact her, write to B.J. Daniels, PO Box 1173, Malta, MT 59538, or email her at bjdaniels@mtintouch.net. Check out her website, www.bjdaniels.com.

Books by B.J. Daniels

*Whitehorse, Montana
%Whitehorse, Montana: The Corbetts
**Whitehorse, Montana: Winchester Ranch
^Whitehorse, Montana: Winchester Ranch Reloaded
+Whitehorse, Montana: Chisholm Cattle Company
&Cardwell Cousins

Other titles by this author available in ebook format.

CAST OF CHARACTERS

Austin Cardwell—The Texan sheriff's deputy found himself in a Montana blizzard with a woman who was either crazy or had good reason to be running scared.

Gillian Cooper—The ID in her purse said her name was Rebecca Stewart, and so did the man claiming to be her husband. So why was she so terrified of Marc Stewart?

Rebecca Stewart—All anyone knew about her was that she had an abusive husband, a young son and a big secret, one that could get her killed.

Marc Stewart—He had the life he'd always dreamed of—until his wife decided she'd had enough.

Victor Ramsey—He had made Marc Stewart into a wealthy man. But now the man was desperate. Victor wasn't sure what Marc would do when cornered.

Dana Cardwell Savage—All she wanted was her family home for Christmas...and to meet her elusive cousin, Austin.

Chapter One

Snow fell in a wall of white, giving Austin Cardwell only glimpses of the winding highway in front of him. He'd already slowed to a crawl as visibility worsened. Now on the radio, he heard that Highway 191 through the Gallatin Canyon—the very one he was on—was closed to all but emergency traffic.

"One-ninety-one from West Yellowstone to Bozeman is closed due to several accidents including a semi rollover that has blocked the highway near Big Sky. Another accident near West Yellowstone has also caused problems there. Travelers are advised to wait out the storm."

Great, Austin thought with a curse. *Wait out the storm where?* He hadn't seen any place to even pull over for miles let alone a gas station or café. He had no choice but to keep going. This was just what this Texas boy needed, he told himself with a curse. He'd be lucky if he reached Cardwell Ranch tonight.

The storm appeared to be getting worse. He couldn't see more than a few yards in front of the rented SUV's hood. Earlier he'd gotten a glimpse of the Gallatin River to his left. On his right were steep rock walls as the two-lane highway cut through the canyon. There was nothing but dark, snow-capped pine trees, steep mountain cliffs and the frozen river and snow-slick highway.

"Welcome to the frozen north," he said under his breath as he fought to see the road ahead—and stay on it. He blamed his brothers—not for the storm, but for his even being here. They had insisted he come to Montana for the grand opening of the first Texas Boys Barbecue joint in Montana. They had postponed the grand opening until he was well enough to come.

Although the opening was to be January 1, his cousin Dana had pleaded with him to spend Christmas at the ranch.

You need to be here, Austin, she'd said. *I promise you won't be sorry.*

He growled under his breath now. He hadn't been back to Montana since his parents divorced and his mother took him and his brothers to Texas to live. He'd been too young to remember much. But he'd found he couldn't say no to Dana. He'd heard too many good things about her from his brothers.

Also, what choice did he have after missing his brother Tag's wedding last July?

As he slowed for another tight curve, a gust of wind shook the rented SUV. Snow whirled past his windshield. For an instant, he couldn't see anything. Worse, he felt as if he was going too fast for the curve. But he was afraid to touch his brakes—the one thing his brother Tag had warned him not to do.

Don't do anything quickly, Tag had told him. *And whatever you do, don't hit your brakes. You'll end up in the ditch.*

He caught something in his headlights. It took him a moment to realize what he was seeing before his heart took off at a gallop.

A car was upside down in the middle of the highway, its headlights shooting out through the falling snow toward the river, the taillights a dim red against the steep canyon wall. The overturned car had the highway completely blocked.

Chapter Two

Austin hit his brakes even though he doubted he stood a chance in hell of stopping. The SUV began to slide sideways toward the overturned car. He spun the wheel, realizing he'd done it too wildly when he began to slide toward the river. As he turned the wheel yet again, the SUV slid toward the canyon wall—and the overturned car.

He was within only a few feet of the car on the road, when his front tires went off the road into the narrow snow-filled ditch between him and the granite canyon wall. The deep snow seemed to grab the SUV and pull it in deeper.

Austin braced himself as snow rushed up over the hood, burying the windshield as the front of the SUV sunk. The ditch and the snow in it were much deeper than he'd thought. He closed his eyes and braced himself for when the SUV hit the steep rock canyon wall.

To his surprise, the SUV came to a sudden stop before it hit the sheer rock face.

He sat for a moment, too shaken to move. Then he remembered the car he'd seen upside down in the middle of the road. What if someone was hurt? He tried his door, but the snow was packed around it. Reaching across the seat, he tried the passenger side. Same problem.

As he sat back, he glanced in the rearview mirror. The rear of the SUV sat higher, the back wheels still partially up on the edge of the highway. He could see out a little of the back window where the snow hadn't blown up on it and realized his only exit would be the hatchback.

He hit the hatchback release then climbed over the seat. In the back, he dug through the clothing he'd brought on the advice of his now "Montana" brother and pulled out the flashlight, along with the winter coat and boots he'd brought. Hurrying, he pulled them on and climbed out through the back into the blinding snowstorm, anxious to see if he could be of any help to the passengers in the wrecked vehicle.

He'd waded through deep snow for a few steps before his feet almost slipped out from under him on the icy highway. No wonder there had been accidents and the highway had closed to all but emergency traffic. The pavement under the falling snow was covered with glare ice. He was amazed he hadn't gone off the road sooner.

Moving cautiously toward the overturned car, he snapped on his flashlight and shone it inside the vehicle, afraid of what he would find.

The driver's seat was empty. So was the passenger seat. The driver's air bag had activated then deflated. In the backseat, though, he saw something that made his pulse jump. A car seat was still strapped in. No baby, though.

He shined the light on the headliner, stopping when he spotted what looked like a woman's purse. Next to it was an empty baby bottle and a smear of blood.

"Hello?" he called out, terrified for the occupants of the car. The night, blanketed by the falling snow, felt too quiet. He was used to Texas traffic and the noise of big-city Houston.

No answer. He had no idea how long ago the accident had happened. Wouldn't the driver have had the good sense to stay nearby? Then again, maybe another vehicle had come from the other side of the highway and rescued the driver and baby. Strange, though, to just leave the car like this without trying to flag the accident.

"Hello?" He listened. He'd never heard such cold silence. It had a spooky quality that made him jumpy. Add to that this car being upside down in the middle of the highway. What if another vehicle came along right now going too fast to stop?

Walking around the car, he found the driver's side door hanging open and bent down to look inside. More blood on the headliner. His heart began to pound even as he told himself someone must have rescued the driver and baby. At least he hoped that was what had happened. But his instincts told him different. While in the barbecue business with his brothers, he worked as a deputy sheriff in a small town outside Houston.

He reached for his cell phone. No service. As he started to straighten, a hard, cold object struck him in the back of the head. Austin Cardwell staggered from the blow and grabbed the car frame to keep from going down. The second blow caught him in the back.

He swung around to ward off another blow.

To his shock, he came face-to-face with a woman wielding a tire iron. But it was the crazed expression on her bloody face that turned his own blood to ice.

Chapter Three

Austin's head swam for a moment as he watched the woman raise the tire iron again. He'd disarmed his fair share of drunks and drugged-up attackers. Now he only took special jobs on a part-time basis, usually the investigative jobs no one else wanted.

Even with his head and back aching from the earlier blows, he reacted instinctively from years of dealing with criminals. He stepped to the side as the woman brought the tire iron down a third time. It connected with the car frame, the sound ringing out an instant before he locked an arm around her neck. With his other hand, he broke her grip on the weapon. It dropped to the ground, disappearing in the falling snow as he dragged her back against him, lifting her off her feet.

Though she was small framed, she proved to be much stronger than he'd expected. She fought as if her life depended on it.

"Settle down," he ordered, his breath coming out as fog in the cold mountain air. "I'm trying to help you."

His words had little effect. He was forced to capture both her wrists in his hands to keep her from striking him as he brought her around to face him.

"Listen to me," he said, putting his face close to hers. "I'm a deputy sheriff from Texas. I'm trying to help you."

She stared at him through the falling snow as if uncomprehending, and he wondered if the injury on her forehead, along with the trauma of the car accident, could be the problem.

"You hit your head when you wrecked your car—"

"It's not my car." She said the words through chattering teeth and he realized that she appeared to be on the verge of hypothermia—something else that could explain her strange behavior.

"Okay, it's not your car. Where is the owner?"

She glanced past him, a terrified expression coming over her face.

"Did you have your baby with you?" he asked.

"I don't have a baby."

The car seat in the back of the vehicle and the baby bottle lying on the headliner next to her purse would indicate otherwise. He hoped, though, that she was telling the truth. He couldn't bear the thought that the baby had come out of the car seat and was somewhere out in the snow.

He listened for a moment. He hadn't heard a baby crying when he'd gotten out of the SUV's hatchback. Nor had he heard one since. The falling snow blanketed everything, though, with that eerie stillness. But he had to assume even if there had been a baby, it wasn't still alive.

He considered what to do. His SUV wasn't coming out of that ditch without a tow truck hooked to it and her car certainly wasn't going anywhere.

"What's your name?" he asked her. She was shaking harder now. He had to get her to someplace warm. Neither of their vehicles was an option. If another vehicle came down this highway from either direction, there was too much of a chance they would be hit. He recalled glimpsing an old boarded-up cabin back up the highway. It wasn't that far. "What's your name?" he asked again.

She looked confused and on the verge of passing out on him. He feared if she did, he wouldn't be able to carry her back to the cabin he'd seen. When he realized he wasn't going to be able to get any information out of her, he reached back into the overturned car and snagged the strap of her purse.

The moment he let go of one of her arms, she tried to run away again and began kicking and clawing at him when he reached for her. He restrained her again, more easily this time because she was losing her motor skills due to the cold.

"We have to get you to shelter. I'm not going to hurt you. Do you understand me?" Any other time, he would have put out some sort of warning sign in case another driver came along. But he couldn't let go of this woman for fear she would attack him again or worse, take off into the storm.

He had to get her to the cabin as quickly as possible. He wasn't sure how badly she was hurt—just that blood was still streaming down her face from the contusion on her forehead. Loss of blood or a concussion could be the cause for her odd behavior. He'd have to restrain her and come back to flag the wreck.

Fortunately, the road was now closed to all but emergency traffic. He figured the first vehicle to come upon the wreck would be highway patrol or possibly a snow-plow driver.

Feeling he had no choice but to get her out of this storm, Austin grabbed his duffel out of the back of the SUV and started to lock it, still holding on to the woman. For the first time, he took a good look at her.

She wore designer jeans, dress boots, a sweater and no

coat. He realized he hadn't seen a winter coat in the car or any snow boots. In her state of mind, she could have removed her coat and left it out in the snow.

Taking off his down coat, he put it on her even though she fought him. He put on the lighter-weight jacket he'd been wearing earlier when he'd gone off the road.

In his duffel bag, he found a pair of mittens he'd invested in before the trip and put them on her gloveless hands, then dug out a baseball cap, the only hat he had. He put it on her head of dark curly hair. The brown eyes staring out at him were wide with fear and confusion.

"You're going to have to walk for a ways," he said to her. She gave him a blank look. But while she appeared more subdued, he wasn't going to trust it. "The cabin I saw from the road isn't far."

It wasn't a long walk. The woman came along without a struggle. But she still seemed terrified of something. She kept looking behind her as they walked as if she feared someone was out there in the storm and would be coming after her. He could feel her body trembling through the grip he had on her arm.

Walking through the falling snow, down the middle of the deserted highway, felt surreal. The quiet, the empty highway, the two of them, strangers, at least one of them in some sort of trouble. It felt as if the world had come to an end and they were the last two people alive.

As they neared where he'd seen the cabin, he hoped his eyes hadn't been deceiving him since he'd only gotten a glimpse through the falling snow. He quickly saw that it was probably only a summer cabin, if that. It didn't look as if it had been used in years. Tiny and rustic, it was set back in a narrow ravine off the highway. The windows had wooden shutters on them and the front door was secured with a padlock.

They slogged through the deep snow up the ravine to the cabin as flakes whirled around them. Austin couldn't remember ever being this cold. The woman had to be freezing since she'd been out in the cold longer than he had and her sweater had to be soaked beneath his coat.

Leading her around to the back, he found a shutter-less window next to the door. Putting his elbow through the old, thin glass, he reached inside and unlocked the door. As he shoved it open, a gust of cold, musty air rushed out.

The woman balked for a moment before he pulled her inside. The room was small, and had apparently once been a porch but was now a storage area. He was relieved to see a stack of dry split wood piled by the door leading into the cabin proper.

Opening the next door, he stepped in, dragging the woman after him. It was pitch-black inside. He dropped his duffel bag and her purse, removed the flashlight from his coat pocket and shone it around the room. An old rock fireplace, the front sooty from years of fires, stood against one wall. A menagerie of ancient furniture formed a half circle around it.

Through a door, he saw one bedroom with a double bed. In another, there were two bunk beds. The bathroom was apparently an outhouse out back. The kitchen was so small he almost missed it.

"We won't have water or any lavatory facilities, but we'll make do since we will have heat as soon as I get a fire going." He looked at her, debating what to do. She couldn't go far inside the small cabin, but she could find a weapon easy enough. He wasn't going to chance it since his head still hurt like hell from the tire iron she'd used to try to cave in his skull. His back was sore, but that was all, fortunately.

Because of his work as a deputy sheriff, he always

carried a gun and handcuffs. He put the duffel bag down on the table, unzipped it and pulled out the handcuffs.

The woman tried to pull free of him at the sight of them.

"Listen," he said gently. "I'm only going to handcuff one of your wrists just to restrain you. I can't trust that you won't hurt me or yourself if I don't." He said all of it apologetically.

Something in his voice must have assured her because she let him lead her over to a chair in front of the fireplace. He snapped one cuff on her right wrist and the other to the frame of the heaviest chair.

She looked around the small cabin, her gaze going to the back door. The terror in her eyes made the hair on the back of his neck spike. He'd once had a girlfriend whose cat used to suddenly look at a doorway as if there were something unearthly standing in it. Austin had the same creepy feeling now and feared that this woman was as haunted as that darned cat.

With the dried wood from the back porch and some matches he found in the kitchen, he got a fire going. Just the sound of the wood crackling and the glow of the flames seemed to instantly warm the room.

He found a pan in the kitchen and, filling it with snow from outside, brought it in and placed it in front of the fire. It wasn't long before he could dampen one end of a dish towel from the kitchen.

"I'm going to wash the blood off your face so I can see how badly you've been hurt, all right?"

She held still as he gently applied the wet towel. The bleeding had stopped over her eye, but it was a nasty gash. It took some searching before he found a first aid kit in one of the bedrooms and bandaged the cut as best he could.

"Are you hurt anywhere else?"

She shook her head.

"Okay," he said with a nod. His head still ached, but the tire iron hadn't broken the skin—only because he had a thick head of dark hair like all of the Cardwells—and a hard head to boot.

The cabin was getting warmer, but he still found an old quilt and wrapped it around her. She had stopped shaking at least. Unfortunately, she still looked confused and scared. He was pretty sure she had a concussion. But there was little he could do. He still had no cell phone coverage. Not that anyone could get to them with the wrecks and the roads the way they were.

Picking up her purse, he sat down in a chair near her. He noticed her watching him closely as he dumped the contents out on the marred wood coffee table. Coins tinkled out, several spilling onto the floor. As he picked them up, he realized several interesting things about what was—and wasn't—in her purse.

There was a whole lot of makeup for someone who didn't have any on. There was also no cell phone. But there *was* a baby's pacifier.

He looked up at her and realized he'd made a rooky mistake. He hadn't searched her. He'd just assumed she didn't have a weapon like a gun or knife because she'd used a tire iron back on the highway.

Getting up, he went over to her and checked her pockets. No cell phone. But he did find a set of car keys. He frowned. That was odd since he remembered that the keys had still been in the wrecked car. The engine had died, but the lights were still on.

So what were these keys for? They appeared to have at least one key for a vehicle and another like the kind used for house doors.

"Are these your keys?" he asked, but after staring at them for a moment, she frowned and looked away.

Maybe she had been telling the truth about the car not being hers.

Sitting back down, he opened her wallet. Three singles, a five—and less than a dollar in change. Not much money for a woman on the road. Not much money dressed like she was either. Also, there were no credit cards.

But there was a driver's license. He pulled it out and looked at the photo. The woman's dark hair in the snapshot was shorter and curlier, but she had the same intense brown eyes. There was enough of a resemblance that he would assume this woman was Rebecca Stewart. According to the ID, she was married, lived in Helena, Montana, and was an organ donor.

"It says here that your name is Rebecca Stewart."

"That's not my purse." She frowned at the bag as if she'd never seen it before.

"Then what was it doing in the car you were driving?"

She shook her head, looking more confused and scared.

"If you're not Rebecca Stewart, then who are you?"

He saw her lower lip quiver. One large tear rolled down her cheek. "I don't know." When she went to wipe her tears with her free hand, he saw the diamond watch.

Reaching over, he caught her wrist. She tried to pull away, but he was much stronger than she was, and more determined. Even at a glance, he could see that the watch was expensive.

"Where did you get this?" he asked, hating that he sounded so suspicious. But the woman had a car and a purse she swore weren't hers. It wasn't that much of a leap to think that the watch probably wasn't hers either.

She stared at the watch on her wrist as if she'd never

seen it before. The gold band was encrusted with diamonds. Pulling it off her wrist, he turned the watch over. Just as he'd suspected, it was engraved:

To Gillian with all my love.

"Is your name Gillian?"

She remembered *something,* he saw it in her eyes.

"So your name *is* Gillian?"

She didn't answer, but now she looked more afraid than she had before.

Austin sighed. He wasn't going to get anything out of this woman. For all he knew, she could be lying about everything. But then again, the fear was real. It was almost palpable.

He had a sudden thought. "Why did you attack me on the highway?"

"I...I don't know."

A chill ran the length of his spine. He thought of how she'd kept looking back at the car as they walked to the cabin. She had thought someone was after her. "Was there someone else in the car when it rolled over?"

Her eyes widened in alarm. "In the trunk."

He gawked at her. *"There was someone in the trunk?"*

She looked confused again, and even more frightened. "No." Tears filled her eyes. "I don't know."

"Too bad you didn't mention that when we were down there," he grumbled under his breath. He couldn't take the chance that she was telling the truth. Why someone would be in the trunk was another concern, especially if she was telling the truth about the car, the purse and apparently the baby not being hers.

He had to go back down anyway and try to put up some kind of flags to warn possible other motorists. He just hated the idea of going back out into the storm. But if there was even a chance someone was in the trunk...

Austin stared at her and reminded himself that this was probably a figment of her imagination. A delusion from the knock on her head. But given the way things weren't adding up, he had to check.

"Don't leave me here," she cried as he headed for the door, her voice filled with terror.

"What are you so afraid of?" he asked, stepping back to her.

She swallowed, her gaze locked with his, and then she slowly shook her head and closed her eyes. "I don't know."

Austin swore under his breath. He didn't like leaving her alone, but he had no choice. He checked to make sure the handcuff attached to the chair would hold in case she tried to go somewhere. He thought it might be just like her, in her state of mind, to get loose and take off back out into the blizzard.

"Don't try to leave, okay? I'll be back shortly. I promise."

She didn't answer, didn't even open her eyes. Grabbing his coat, he hurried out the back door and down the steep slope to the highway. The snow lightened the dark enough that he didn't have to use his flashlight. It was still falling in huge lacy flakes that stuck to his clothing as he hurried down the highway. He wished he'd at least taken his heavier coat from her before he'd left.

His SUV was covered with snow and barely visible. He walked past it to the overturned car, trying to make sense of all this. Someone in the trunk? He mentally kicked himself for worrying about some crazy thing a delusional woman had said.

The car was exactly as he'd left it, although the lights were starting to dim, the battery no doubt running down. He thought about turning them off, but if a car came along, the driver would have a better chance of seeing it with the lights on.

He went around to the driver's side. The door was still open, just as he'd left it. He turned on the flashlight from his pocket and searched around for the latch on the trunk, hoping he wouldn't have to use the key, which was still in the ignition.

Maybe it was the deputy sheriff in him, but he had a bad feeling this car might be the scene of a crime and whoever's fingerprints were on the key might be important.

He found the latch. The trunk made a soft *thunk* and fell open.

Austin didn't know what he expected to find when he walked around to the back of the car and bent down to look in. A body? Or a woman and her baby?

What had fallen out, though, was only a suitcase.

He stared at it for a moment, then knelt down and unzipped it enough to see what was inside. Clothes. Women's clothing. No dead bodies. Nothing to be terrified of that he could see.

The bag, though, had been packed quickly, the clothes apparently just thrown in. That in itself was interesting. Nor did the clothing look expensive—unlike the diamond wristwatch the woman was wearing.

Checking the luggage tag on the bag, he saw that it was in the same name as the driver's license he'd found in her purse. Rebecca Stewart. So if Rebecca Stewart wasn't the woman in the cabin, then where was she? And where was the baby who went with the car seat?

He rezipped the bag and hoisted it up from the snow. Was the woman going to deny that this was her suitcase? He reminded himself that she'd thought there was *someone* in the trunk. The woman obviously wasn't in her right mind.

He shone the flashlight into the trunk. His pulse quickened. Blood. He removed a glove to touch a finger to it. Dried. What the hell? There wasn't much, but enough to cause even more concern.

Putting his glove back on, he closed the trunk and picked up the suitcase. He stopped at his rented SUV to look for something to flag the wreck, hurrying because he was worried about the woman, worried what he would find when he got back to the cabin. He was digging in the back of the SUV, when a set of headlights suddenly flashed over him.

He turned. Out of the storm came the flashing lights of a Montana highway patrol car.

Chapter Four

"Let me get this straight," the patrolman said as they stood in the waiting room at the hospital. "You handcuffed her to a chair to protect her from herself?"

"Some of it was definitely for my own protection, as well. She appeared confused and scared. I couldn't trust that she wouldn't go for a more efficient weapon than a tire iron."

The patrolman finished writing and closed his notebook. "Unless you want to press assault charges...that should cover it."

Austin shook his head. "How is she?"

"The doctor is giving her liquids and keeping her for observation until we can reach her husband."

"Her husband?" Austin thought of the hurriedly packed suitcase and recalled that she hadn't been wearing a wedding ring.

"We tracked him down through the car registration."

"So she *is* Rebecca Stewart? Her memory has returned?"

"Not yet. But I'm sure her husband will be able to clear things up." The patrolman stood. "I have your number if we need to reach you."

Austin stood, as well. He was clearly being dismissed and yet something kept him from turning and walking away. "She seemed…terrified when I found her. Did she say where she was headed before the crash?"

"She still seems fuzzy on that part. But she is in good hands now." The highway patrolman turned as the doctor came down the hallway and joined them. "Mr. Cardwell is worried about your patient. I assured him she is out of danger," the patrolman said.

The doctor nodded and introduced himself to Austin. "If it makes you feel better, there is little doubt you saved her life."

He couldn't help but be relieved. "Then she remembers what happened?"

"She's still confused. That's fairly common in a case like hers."

The doctor didn't say, but Austin assumed she had a concussion. Austin couldn't explain why, but he needed to see her before he left. The highway patrolman had said they'd found her husband by way of the registration in the car, but she'd been so sure that wasn't her car.

Nor had the highway patrolman been concerned about the baby car seat or the blood in the trunk.

"Apparently the baby is with the father," the patrolman had told him. "As for the blood in the trunk, there was so little I'm sure there is an explanation her husband can provide."

So why couldn't Austin let it go? "I'd like to see her before I leave."

"I suppose it would be fine," the doctor said. "Her husband is expected at any time."

Austin hurried down the hallway to the room the doctor had only exited moments before, anxious to see her before her husband arrived. He pushed on the door slowly and peered in, half fearing that she might not want to see him.

He wasn't sure what he expected as he stepped into the room. He'd had a short sleepless night at a local motel. He had regretted not taking a straight flight to Bozeman this morning instead of flying into Idaho Falls the day before. Even as he thought it through, he reminded himself that the woman would have died last night if he hadn't come along when he did.

Austin told himself he'd been at the right place at the right time. So why couldn't he just let this go?

As the door closed behind him, she sat up in bed abruptly, pulling the covers up to her chin.

Her brown eyes were wide with fear. He was struck by how small she looked. Her unruly mane of curly dark hair billowed out around her pale face, making her look all the more vulnerable.

"My name's Austin. Austin Cardwell. We met late last night after I came upon your car upside down in the middle of Highway 191." He touched the wound on the back of his head where she'd nailed him. "You remember hitting me?"

She looked horrified at the thought, verifying what he already suspected. She didn't remember.

"Can you tell me your name?" He'd hoped that she would be more coherent this morning, but as he watched her face, it was clear she didn't know who she was any more than she had last night.

She seemed to search for an answer. He saw the moment when she realized she couldn't remember anything—even who she was. Panic filled her expression. She looked toward the door behind him as if she might bolt for it.

"Don't worry," he said quickly. "The doctor said memory loss is pretty common in your condition."

"My *condition?*"

"From the bump on your head, you hit it pretty hard in the accident." He pointed to a spot on his own temple. She raised her hand to touch the same spot on her temple and winced.

"I don't remember an accident." She had pulled her arms out from under the covers. He noticed the bruises on her upper arms. They were half-moon shaped, like fingerprints—as if someone had gripped her hard. There was also a cut on her arm that he didn't think had happened during her car accident.

She saw him staring at her arms. When she looked down and saw the bruises, she quickly put her arms under the covers again. If anything, she looked more frightened than she had earlier.

"You don't remember losing control of your car?"

She shook her head.

"I don't know if this helps, but the registration and proof of insurance I found in your car, along with the driver's license I found in the purse, says your name is Rebecca Stewart," he said, watching to see if there was any recognition in her expression.

"That isn't my name. I would know my own name when I heard it, wouldn't I?"

Maybe. Maybe not. "You were wearing a watch…"

"The doctor said they put it in the safe until I was ready to leave the hospital."

"It was engraved with: 'To Gillian with all my love.'" He saw that the words didn't ring any bells. "Are you Gillian?"

She looked again at the door, her expression one of panic.

"Don't worry. It will all come back to you," he said, trying to calm her even though he knew there might always be blanks that she could never fill in if he was right and she had a concussion. He wished there was something he could say to comfort her. She looked so frightened. "Fortunately a highway patrolman came along when he did last night."

"Patrolman?" Her words wavered and she looked even more terrified, making him wonder if he might be right and that she'd stolen the car, the purse and the watch. She'd said none of it belonged to her. Maybe she *was* telling the truth.

But why was she driving someone else's car? If so, where was the car's owner and her baby? This woman's fear of the law seemed to indicate that something was very off here. What if this woman wasn't who they thought she was?

"Where am I?" she asked, glancing around the hospital room.

"Didn't the doctor tell you? You're in the hospital."

"I meant, where am I…?" She waved a hand to encompass more than the room.

"Oh," he said and frowned. "Bozeman." When that didn't seem to register, he added, "Montana."

One eyebrow shot up. *"Montana?"*

It crossed his mind that a woman who lived in Helena, Montana, wouldn't be confused about what state she was in. Nor would she be surprised to find herself still in that state.

He reminded himself that the knock on her head could have messed up some of the wiring. Or maybe she'd been that way before.

Her gaze came back to him. She was studying him intently, sizing him up. He wondered what she saw and couldn't help but think of his former girlfriend, Tanya, and the argument they'd had just before he'd left Texas.

"Haven't you ever wanted more?" Tanya hadn't looked

at him. She'd been busy throwing her things into a large trash bag. When she'd moved in with him, she'd moved in gradually, bringing her belongings in piecemeal.

"I'm only going to be gone a week," he'd said, watching her clean out the drawers in his apartment, wondering if this was it. She'd threatened to leave him enough times, but she never had. Maybe this was the time.

He had been trying to figure out how he felt about that when she'd suddenly turned toward him.

"Did you hear what I said?"

Obviously not. *"What?"*

"This business with your brothers..." She did her eye roll. He really hated it when she did that and she knew it. *"If it isn't something to do with* Texas Boys Barbecue*..."*

He could have pointed out that the barbecue joint she was referring to was a multimillion-dollar business, with more than a dozen locations across Texas, and it paid for this apartment.

But he'd had a feeling that wasn't really what this particular argument was about, so he'd said, *"Your point?"* even though he'd already known it.

"You're too busy for a relationship. At least that is your excuse."

"You knew I was busy before you moved in."

"Ever ask yourself why your work is more important than your love life?" She hadn't given him time to respond. *"You want to know what I think? I think Austin Cardwell goes through life saving people because he's afraid of letting himself fall in love."*

He wasn't afraid. He just hadn't fallen in love the way Tanya had wanted him to. *"Glad we got that figured out,"* he'd said.

Tanya had flared with anger. *"That's all you have to say?"*

And he'd made it worse by shrugging, something he knew *she* hated. He hadn't had the time or patience for this kind of talk at that moment. *"Maybe we should talk about this when I get back from Montana."*

She'd shaken her head in obvious disgust. *"That is so like you. Put things off and maybe the situation will right itself. You missed your own brother's wedding and you don't really care if they open a barbecue restaurant in Montana or not. But instead of being honest, you ignore the problem and hope it goes away until finally they force you to come to Montana. For once, I would love to see you just take a stand. Make a decision. Do something."*

"I missed my brother's wedding because I was on a case. One that almost got me killed, you might remember."

Tears welled in her eyes. *"I remember. I stayed by your bedside for three days."*

He sighed and raked a hand through his hair. *"What I do is important."*

"More important than me." She'd stood, hands on hips, waiting.

He'd known what she wanted. A commitment. The problem was, he wasn't ready. And right then, he'd known he would never be with Tanya.

"This is probably for the best," he'd said, motioning to the bulging trash bag.

Tears flowing, she'd nodded. *"Don't bother to call me if and when you get back."* With that, she had grabbed up the bag and stormed to the door, stopping only long enough to hurl his apartment key at his head.

"Where are my clothes?"

Austin blinked, confused for a moment, he'd been so lost in his thoughts. He focused on the woman in the hospital bed. "You can't leave. Your husband is on his way."

Panic filled her expression. She tried to get out of the bed. As he moved to her bedside to stop her, he heard the door open behind him.

Chapter Five

Austin turned to see a large stocky man come into the room, followed by the doctor.

"Mrs. Stewart," the doctor said as he approached her bed. "Your husband is here."

The stocky man stopped a few feet into the room and stood frowning. For a moment, Austin thought there had been a mistake and that the man didn't recognize the woman.

But the man wasn't looking at his wife. He was frowning at Austin. As if the doctor's words finally jarred him into motion, the man strode to the other side of the bed and quickly took his wife's hand as he bent to kiss her forehead. "I was so worried about you."

Austin watched the woman's expression. She looked terrified, her gaze locking with his in a plea for help.

"Excuse me," Austin said as he stepped forward. He had no idea what he planned to say, let alone do. But something was wrong here.

"I beg your pardon?" said the alleged husband, turning to look at Austin before swinging his gaze to the doctor with a *who the hell is this?* expression.

"This is the man who saved your wife's life," the doctor said and introduced Austin before getting a page that he was needed elsewhere. He excused himself and hurried out, leaving the three of them alone.

"I'm sorry, I didn't catch your name," Austin said.

"Marc. Marc Stewart."

Stewart, Austin thought, remembering the name on the driver's license in the purse he'd found in the car. "And this woman's name is Rebecca Stewart?" he asked the husband.

"That's right," Marc Stewart answered in a way that dared Austin to challenge him.

As he looked to the woman in the bed, Austin noticed that she gave an almost imperceptible shake of her head. "I'm sorry, but how do we know you're her husband?"

"Are you serious?" the man demanded, glaring across the bed at him.

"She doesn't seem to recognize you," he said, even though what he'd noticed was that the woman seemed terrified of the man.

Marc Stewart gave him the once-over, clearly upset. "She's had a *concussion.*"

"Old habits are hard to break," Austin said as he displayed his badge and ID to the alleged Marc Stewart. "You wouldn't mind me asking for some identification from you, would you?"

The man looked as if he might have a coronary. At least he'd come to the right place, Austin thought, as the alleged Marc Stewart angrily pulled out his wallet and showed Austin his license.

Marc Andrew Stewart, Austin read. "There was a car seat in the back of the vehicle she was driving. Where is the baby?"

"With my mother." A blood vessel in the man's cheek began to throb. "Look Deputy…Cardwell, is it? I appreciate that you supposedly saved my wife's life, but it's time for you to butt out."

Austin told himself he should back off, but the fear in the woman's eyes wouldn't let him. "She doesn't seem to know you and she isn't wearing a wedding ring." He didn't add that the woman seemed terrified and had bruises on her upper arms where someone had gotten rough with her. Not to mention the fact that when he'd told her that her husband was on his way, she'd panicked and tried to leave. Concussion or not, something was wrong with all this.

"I think you should leave," the man said.

"If you really are her husband, it shouldn't be hard for you to prove it," Austin said, holding his ground—well, at least until Marc Stewart had hospital security throw him out, which wouldn't be long, from the look on the man's face. The woman in the bed still hadn't uttered a word.

For a moment, Marc Stewart looked as if he was about to tell him to go to hell. But instead, he dug into his pocket angrily and produced a plain gold band that caught the light as he reached for the woman's left hand.

"My wife left it by the sink yesterday," Marc Stewart said by way of explanation. "She always takes it off when she does the dishes. Sometimes she forgets to put it back on."

Austin thought, given the bruises on the woman's upper arms, that she had probably thrown the ring at him as she took off yesterday.

When she still didn't move to take the ring, the man snatched up her hand lying beside her on the bed and slipped the ring on her finger.

Austin watched her look down at the ring. He saw recognition fill her expression just before she began to cry. Even from where he stood, he could see that the ring, while a little loose, fit close enough. Just as the photo ID in Rebecca Stewart's purse looked enough like the woman on the bed. He told himself there was nothing more he could do. Clearly she was afraid of this man. But unless she spoke up…

"I guess I'll leave you with your husband, unless there is something I should know?" Austin asked her.

"Tell the man, Rebecca," Marc Stewart snapped. "Am I your husband?" He bent down to kiss her cheek. Austin saw him whisper something in her ear.

She closed her eyes, tears leaking from beneath dark lashes.

"We had a little argument and she took off and apparently almost got herself killed," Marc said. "We both said and did things we regret, isn't that right, Rebecca? Tell the man, sweetheart."

Her eyes opened slowly. She took a ragged breath and wiped away the tears with the backs of her hands, the way a little kid would.

"Is that all there is to this?" Austin asked, watching her face. Across from him, he could see Marc gritting his teeth in fury at this interference in his life.

She nodded her head slowly, her gaze going from her husband to Austin. "Thank you, but he's right. It was just a foolish disagreement. I will be fine now."

FEELING LIKE A fool for getting involved in a domestic dispute, Austin headed for Cardwell Ranch. Last night, a wrecker company had pulled his rental SUV out of the ditch and brought it to the motel where he was staying. Fortunately, his skid into the ditch hadn't done any damage.

Highway 191 was now open, the road sanded. As he drove, Austin got his first real look at the Gallatin

Canyon or "the canyon" as his cousin Dana called it. From the mouth just south of Gallatin Gateway, fifty miles of winding road trailed the river in a deep cut through the mountains, almost all the way to West Yellowstone.

The drive along the Gallatin River was indeed breathtaking—a snaking strip of highway followed the Blue Ribbon trout stream up over the Continental Divide. This time of year, the Gallatin ran crystal clear under a thick cover of aquamarine ice. Dark, thick snowcapped pines grew at its edge, against a backdrop of the granite cliffs and towering pine-clad mountains.

Austin concentrated on his driving so he didn't end up in a snowbank again. Piles of deep snow had been plowed up on each side of the road, making the highway seem even narrower, but at least traffic was light. He had to admit, it was beautiful. The sun glistening off the new snow was almost blinding in its brilliance. Overhead, a cloudless robin's-egg-blue sky seemed vast and clearer than any air he'd ever breathed. The canyon looked like something out of a winter fairy tale.

Just before Big Sky, the canyon widened a little. He spotted a few older cabins, nothing like all the new construction he'd seen down by the mouth of the canyon. Tag had told him that the canyon had been mostly cattle and dude ranches, a few summer cabins and homes— that was, until Big Sky resort and the small town that followed at the foot of Lone Mountain.

Luxury houses had sprouted up all around the resort. Fortunately, some of the original cabins still remained and the majority of the canyon was national forest so it would always remain undeveloped. The "canyon" had remained its own little community, according to Tag.

Austin figured Tag had gotten most of his information

from their cousin Dana. This was the only home she'd known and, like her stubborn relations, she apparently had no intention of ever leaving it.

While admiring the scenery on the drive, he did his best not to think about Rebecca Stewart and her husband. When he'd left her hospital room, he'd felt her gaze on him and turned at the door to look back. He'd seen her take off the ring her husband had put on her finger and grip it in her fist so tightly that her knuckles were white.

Trouble in paradise, he thought as he reached Big Sky, *and none of my business.* As a deputy sheriff, he'd dealt with his share of domestic disputes. Every law enforcement officer knew how dangerous they were. The best thing was to stay out of the middle of them since he'd seen both husbands and wives turn on the outsider stepping in to try to keep the peace.

Cardwell Ranch was only a few miles farther up the highway from Big Sky. But on impulse, he swung onto the road to Big Sky's Meadow Village, where he suspected he would find the marshal's department.

His cousin Dana's husband, Marshal Hud Savage, waved him into his office and shook his hand. "We missed you at the wedding." The wedding, of course, had been his brother Tag's, to Lily McCabe, on July 4. He knew he would never live it down.

"I was hoping to get up for it, but I was on a case…" He hated that he'd missed his own brother's wedding, but hoped at least Hud, being a lawman, would understand.

"That's right. Deputy sheriff, is it?"

"Part-time, yes. I take on special cases."

"As I recall, there were extenuating circumstances. You were wounded. You're fine now?"

He nodded. He didn't want to talk about the case that

had almost gotten him killed. Nor did he want to admit that he might not still be physically a hundred percent.

"Well, have a seat," Hud said as he settled behind his desk. "And tell me what I can do for you. I suspect this isn't an extended family visit."

Austin nodded and, removing his hat, sat down, comfortable at once with the marshal. "You might have heard that I got into an accident last night. My rental SUV went into the ditch."

"I did know about that. I'm glad you weren't hurt. We couldn't assist because we had our hands full down here with a semi rollover."

"I was lucky I only ended up in the ditch. What made me hit my brakes was that I came upon a vehicle upside down in the middle of the highway last night."

Austin filled him in on the woman and everything that had happened up to leaving her about thirty minutes ago at the hospital in Bozeman.

"Sounds like she and her husband were having some marital issues," the marshal said.

Austin nodded. "The trouble is I think it's more than that. She had bruises on her arms."

"Couldn't the bruises have been caused by the accident?"

"No, these were definitely finger impressions. More than that, she seemed scared of her husband. Actually, she told me she wasn't Rebecca Stewart, which would mean this man wasn't her husband." He saw skepticism in the marshal's expression and admitted he would have felt the same way if someone had come to him with this story.

"Look," Austin said. "It's probably nothing, but I just have this gut feeling…"

Hud nodded, as if he understood gut feelings. "What would you like me to do?"

"First, could you run the name Marc Stewart. They're apparently from Helena."

"If it will relieve your mind, I'd be happy to." The marshal moved to his computer and began to peck at the keys. A moment later, he said, "No arrests or warrants. None on Rebecca Stewart either. Other than that…"

Austin nodded.

Hud studied him. "There's obviously something that's still worrying you."

He couldn't narrow it down to just one thing. It was the small things like the older-model car Rebecca had been driving, the baby seat in the back, the woman's adamant denial that she was Rebecca Stewart, the look of fear on her face when he'd told her that her husband was on his way to the hospital, the way she'd cried when he'd put that ring back on her finger.

Then there was that expensive diamond watch. *To Gillian with all my love.*

He mentioned all of this to the marshal and added, "I guess what's really bothering me is the inconsistencies. Also she just doesn't seem like the kind of woman who would leave her husband—let alone her baby—right before Christmas, no matter what the argument might have been about. This woman is a fighter. She wouldn't have left her son with a man who had just gotten physical with her."

Hud raised a brow as he leaned back in his chair. "You sure you didn't get a little too emotionally involved?"

He laughed. "Not hardly. Haven't you heard? I'm the Cardwell brother who never gets emotionally involved in anything. Just ask my brothers, or my former girlfriend, for that matter." He hesitated even though common sense told him to let it go. "There's no chance you're going into Bozeman today, is there?"

Hud smiled. "I'll stop by the hospital and give you a call after I talk to her and her husband."

"Thanks. It really would relieve my mind." Glancing at his watch, he saw he was late for a meeting with his brothers.

He swore as he hurried outside, climbed behind the wheel of his rental SUV and drove toward the small strip shopping mall in Meadow Village, all the time worrying about the woman he'd left in the hospital.

THE BUILDING WAS wood framed with stone across the front. It looked nothing like a Texas barbecue joint. As Austin climbed out of the SUV and walked through the snow toward the end unit with the Texas Boys Barbecue sign out front, he thought of their first barbecue joint.

It had been in an old small house. They'd done the barbecuing out back and packed diners in every afternoon and evening at mismatched tables and chairs to eat on paper plates. Just the smell of the wonderfully smoked meats brought people in. He and his brothers didn't even have to advertise. Their barbecue had kept people coming back for more.

Austin missed those days, sitting out back having a cold beer after the night was over and counting their money and laughing at what a fluke it had been. They'd grown up barbecuing so it hadn't felt like work at all.

As he pushed open the door to the building his brothers had bought, he saw by the way it was laid out that the space had started out as another restaurant. Whatever had been here, though, had been replaced with the Texas Boys Barbecue decor, a mix of rustic wood and galvanized aluminum. The fabric of the cushy red booths was the same as that on the chairs, and red-checked tablecloths covered the tables. The walls were covered with old photos of Texas family barbecues—just like in their other restaurants.

Through the pass-through he could see a gleaming kitchen at the back. Hearing his brothers—Tag, Jackson, Laramie and Hayes—visiting back there, he walked in that direction.

"Well, what do you think?" Tag asked excitedly.

Austin shrugged. "It looks fine."

"The equipment is all new," Jackson said. "We had to add a few things, but other than that, the remodel was mostly cosmetic."

Austin nodded. "What happened to the restaurant that was here?"

"It didn't serve the best barbecue in Texas," Tag said.

"We'd hoped for a little more enthusiasm," Laramie said.

"Sorry."

"What about the space?" Hayes asked.

"Looks good to me." He saw them share a glance at each other before they laughed and, almost in unison, said, "Same ol' Austin."

He didn't take offense. It was actually good to see his brothers. There was no mistaking they were related either since they'd all inherited the Cardwell dark good looks. A curse and a blessing. When they were teens they used to argue over who was the ugliest. He smiled at the memory.

"Okay, we're opening a Texas Boys Barbecue in Big Sky," he said to them. "So buy me some lunch. I'm starved."

They went to a small sandwich shop in the shadow of Lone Mountain in what was called Mountain Village. As hungry as he was, Austin still had trouble getting down even half of a sandwich and a bowl of soup.

During lunch, his brothers talked enthusiastically

about the January 1 opening. They planned two grand openings, one on January 1 and another on July 4, since Big Sky had two distinct tourist seasons.

Apparently the entire canyon was excited about the Cardwell brothers' brand of barbecue. His brothers Tag, Hayes and Jackson now had all made their homes in Montana. Only he and Laramie still lived in Texas, but Laramie would be flying back up for the grand opening whenever that schedule was confirmed. None of them asked if Austin would be coming back for that one. They knew him too well.

Austin only half listened, too anxious for a call from the marshal. When his cell phone finally did ring, he quickly excused himself and went out to the closed-in deck. It was freezing out here, but he didn't want his brothers to hear. He could actually see his breath. He'd never admit it, but he couldn't imagine why they would want to live here, as cold and nasty as winter was. Sure, it was beautiful, but he'd take Texas and the heat any day.

"I just left her hospital room," the marshal said without preamble the moment Austin answered.

"So what do you think?"

"Apparently she has some loss of memory because of the concussion she suffered, according to her husband, which could explain some of your misgivings."

"Did you see the bruises on her arms?"

The marshal sighed. "I did. Her husband said they'd had a disagreement before she took off. He said he'd grabbed her a little too hard, trying to keep her from leaving, afraid in her state what might happen to her. As it was, she ended up in a car wreck."

"What does she say?"

"She doesn't seem to recall the twenty-four hours

before ending up upside down in her car in the middle of the highway—and even that is fuzzy."

"You think she's lying?" Austin asked, hearing something in the marshal's voice.

Hud took his time in answering. "I think she might remember more than she's letting on. I had some misgivings as well until Marc Stewart showed me a photograph of the four of them on his cell phone."

"*Four* of them?"

"Rebecca and her sister, a woman named Gillian Cooper, Marc and the baby. In the photo, the woman in the hospital is holding the baby and Marc is standing next to her, his arm around her and her sister."

Austin sighed. Gillian Cooper. Her sister. That could explain the watch. Maybe her sister had lent it to her. Or even given it to her.

"The doctor is releasing her tomorrow. I asked her if she wanted to return home with her husband."

Austin figured he already knew the answer. "She said yes."

"I also asked him to step out of the room. I then asked her if she was afraid of him. She said she wasn't."

So that was that, Austin thought. "Thanks for going by the hospital for me."

"You realize there is nothing we can do if she doesn't want to leave him," Hud said.

Austin knew that from experience, even though he'd never understood why a woman stayed in an abusive marriage. Disconnecting, he went back into the restaurant, where his brothers were debating promotion for the new restaurant. He was in no mood for this.

"I really should get going," he said, not that he really had anywhere to go, though he'd agreed to stay until the opening.

Christmas was only a few days away, he realized. Normally, he didn't do much for Christmas. Since he didn't have his own family, he always volunteered to work.

"Where are you going?" Tag asked.

"I've got some Christmas shopping to do." That, at least, was true.

"Dana is planning for us all to be together on Christmas," Tag said as if he needed reminding. "She has all kinds of plans."

Jackson laughed. "She wants us all to try skiing or snowboarding."

"There's a sledding party planned on Christmas Eve behind the house on the ranch and, of course, ice skating on an inlet of the Gallatin River," Hayes said with a laugh when he saw Austin's expression. "You really have to experience a Montana Christmas."

He tried to smile. Anything to make up for missing the wedding so everyone would quit bringing it up. "I can't wait."

They all laughed since they knew he was lying. He wasn't ready for a Montana Christmas. He'd already been freezing his butt off and figured he'd more than experienced Montana after crashing in a ditch and almost getting killed by a woman with a tire iron. However, never let it be said he was a Scrooge. He'd go Christmas shopping. He would be merry and bright. It was only for a few days.

"You know what your problem is, Austin?" his brother Jackson said as they walked out to their vehicles.

Austin shook his head although he knew what was coming. He'd already had this discussion with Tanya in Houston.

"You can't commit to anything," Jackson said. "When we decided to open more Texas Boys Barbecues in Texas—"

"Yes, I've been told I have a problem with commitment," he interrupted as he looked toward Lone Mountain. The peak was almost completely obscured by the falling snow. Huge lacy flakes drifted down around them. Texas barbecue in Montana? He'd thought his brothers had surely lost their minds when they had suggested it. Now he was all the more convinced.

But they'd been right about the other restaurants they'd opened across Texas. He wasn't going to stand in their way now. But he also couldn't get all that excited about it.

"Can you at least commit to this promotion schedule we have mapped out?" Hayes asked.

"Do what you think is best," he said, opening the SUV door. "I'll go along with whatever y'all decide." His brothers didn't look thrilled with his answer. "Isn't that what you wanted me to say?"

"We were hoping for some enthusiasm, *something*," Jackson said and frowned. "You seem to have lost interest in the business."

"It's not that." It wasn't. It was his *life*. At thirty-two, he was successful, a healthy, wealthy American male who could do anything he wanted. Most men his age would have given anything to be in his boots.

"He needs a woman," Tag said and grinned.

"That's *all* I need," Austin said sarcastically under his breath and thought of Rebecca and the way she'd reacted to her husband. What kind of woman left her husband and child just before Christmas?

A terrified one, he thought. "I have to go."

"Where did you say you were going?" Hayes asked before Austin could close his SUV door.

"There's something I need to do."

"I told you he needed a woman," Tag joked.

"Dana is in Bozeman running errands, but she said to

tell you that dinner is at her house tonight," Jackson said before Austin could escape.

All the way to the hospital in Bozeman, all Austin could think about was the woman he'd rescued last night. Rescued? And then turned her over to a man who terrified her.

Austin thought of that awful old expression: she'd made her bed and now she had to lie in it.

Like hell, he thought.

Chapter Six

When he reached the hospital, Austin was told at the nurses' station that Mrs. Stewart had checked out already. His heart began to pound harder at the news, all his instincts telling him he had been right to come back here.

"I thought the doctor wasn't going to release her until tomorrow?"

"Her husband talked to him and asked if she was well enough to be released. He was anxious to get her home before Christmas."

Austin just bet he was. "He was planning to take her straight home from the hospital?" he asked and quickly added, "I have her purse." He'd forgotten all about putting it into his duffel bag last night as the highway patrolman helped the woman down to his waiting patrol car.

"Oh, you must be the man who found her after the accident," the nurse said, instantly warming toward him. "Let me see. I know her husband stayed at a local motel last night. I believe they were going to go there first so she could rest for a while before they left for Helena."

"Her husband got in last night?" Austin asked in surprise. Helena was three hours away on Interstate 90.

"He arrived in the wee hours of the morning. When he came by the hospital to see his wife, he thought he'd be able to take her home then." She smiled at how anxious the husband had apparently been. "He left the name of the motel where he would stay if there was any change in her condition," the nurse said. "Here it is. The Pine Rest. I can call and see if they are still there."

"No, that's all right. I'll run by the motel." He realized Rebecca Stewart wouldn't have been allowed to walk out of the hospital. One of the nurses would have taken her down to the car by wheelchair. "You don't happen to know what Mr. Stewart was driving, do you?" She remembered the large black Suburban because it had looked brand-new.

The Pine Rest Motel sat on the east end of town on a hill. Austin spotted Marc Stewart's Suburban at once. Austin had to wonder why Marc's "wife" had been driving an older model car.

That didn't surprise him as much as the lack of a baby car seat in the back of the Suburban. Marc had had the vehicle for almost a month according to the sticker in the back window. The lack of a car seat was just another one of those questions that nagged at him. Like the fact that Marc Stewart had gotten his wife out of the hospital early just to bring her to a motel in town. That made no sense unless he'd brought her there to threaten her. That Austin could believe.

The black Suburban was parked in front of motel unit number seven—the last unit at the small motel.

Austin didn't go anywhere without his weapon. But he knew better than to go into the motel armed—let alone without a plan. He tended to wing things, following his instincts. It had gotten him this far. But it had also nearly gotten him killed last summer. He had both the physical and mental scars to prove it.

Glancing at the purse lying on the seat next to him, he wondered if all this wasn't an overreaction on his part.

Maybe it had only been an argument between husband and wife that had gotten out of control. Maybe once Rebecca Stewart's memory returned, she wouldn't be afraid of her husband.

Maybe.

He picked up the purse. It was imitation leather, a knockoff of a famous designer's. He pulled out the wallet and went through it again, this time noticing the discount coupons for diapers and groceries.

He studied the woman in the photo a second time. It wasn't a great snapshot of her, but then most driver's license mug shots weren't. Montana only required a driver to get a license every eight years so this photo was almost seven years old.

If it hadn't been for the slight resemblance… He put everything back into the purse, opened the car door and stepped out into the falling snow.

Every cop knew not to get in the middle of a domestic dispute. This wasn't like him, he thought as he walked through the storm to the door of unit number seven and knocked.

At his knock, Austin heard a scurrying sound. He knocked again. A few moments later, Marc Stewart opened the door a crack.

He frowned when he saw Austin. "Yes?"

"I'm Austin Cardwell—"

"I know who you are." Behind the man, Austin heard a sound.

"I forgot to give Rebecca her purse," he said.

Marc reached for it.

All his training told him to just hand the man the damned purse and walk away. It wasn't like him to butt into someone else's business—let alone a married couple's, even if they had some obvious problems—when he wasn't asked.

"If you don't mind, I'd like to give it to her myself," he heard himself say. Behind the man, Austin caught a rustling sound.

"Look," Marc Stewart said from between gritted teeth. "I appreciate that you found…my wife and kept her safe until I could get here, but your job is done, cowboy. So you need to back the hell off."

Rebecca suddenly appeared at the man's side. "Excuse my husband. He's just upset." She met Austin's gaze. He tried to read it, afraid she was desperately trying to tell him something. "But Marc's right. We're fine now. It was very thoughtful of you to bring my purse, though."

"Yes, thoughtful," Marc said sarcastically and shot his wife a warning look. "You shouldn't be up," he snapped.

She was pale and a little unsteady on her feet, but she had a determined look on her face. Behind her, he saw her open suitcase—the same one he'd found in the overturned car's trunk. The scene looked like any other married couple's motel room.

Even before Marc spoke, Austin realized they were about to pack up and leave.

"We were just heading out," Marc said.

"I won't keep you, then," Austin said, still holding the purse. Rebecca Stewart looked weak as she leaned into the door frame. He feared her husband had gotten her out of the hospital too soon. But that, too, was none of his business. "I didn't want you leaving without your purse."

"Great," Marc said and turned to close her suitcase. "We have a long drive ahead of us, so if you'll excuse us…" Austin stepped aside to let him pass with the suitcase. "You should tell him our good news," he called over his shoulder.

"Good news?" Austin asked, studying the woman in the doorway. He realized that even though her suitcase had been open, she was still wearing the same clothing she'd had on last night. That realization gave him a start since there was a spot of blood on her sweater from her head injury the night before.

"We're pregnant again," Marc called from the side of the Suburban, where he was loading the suitcase.

Austin was watching her face. She suddenly went paler. He thought for a moment that she might faint.

"Marc, don't—" The words came out like a plea.

"Andrew Marc, our son, is going to have a baby sister," Marc said as if he hadn't heard her or was ignoring her. "Isn't that right, Rebecca? I think we'll call her Becky."

Austin met her gaze. "Congratulations." He couldn't have felt more like a fool as he handed her the purse.

She took it with trembling fingers, her eyes filling with tears. "Thank you for bringing my purse all this way." Her fingers kneaded the cheap fabric of the bag. He saw she was again wearing the wedding band that her husband had put on her finger at the hospital. That alone should have told him how things were.

"No problem. Good luck." He meant it since he knew in his heart she was going to need it. He started to step away when she suddenly grabbed his arm.

"Wait, I think this must be your coat," she said and turned back into the room.

"That's okay, you should keep it," he said.

She returned a few moments later with the coat.

"Seriously, keep it. You need it more than I do."

"Take the damned coat," Marc called to him before slamming the Suburban door.

Austin shook his head at her. "Keep it. Please," he said quietly.

Tears filled her eyes. "Thank you." She quickly reached for his hand and pressed what felt like a scrap of paper into his palm. "For everything." She then quickly pulled down her shirtsleeve, which had ridden up. He only got a glimpse of the fresh red mark around her wrist.

Austin sensed Marc behind him as he helped her into his coat. It swallowed her, but the December day was cold, another snowstorm threatening.

"Well, if we've all wished each other enough luck, it's time to hit the road," Marc said, joining them. "Hormones." He sounded disgusted as he looked at his wife. "The woman is in tears half the time." He put one arm around her roughly and reached into his pocket with the other. "Forgive my manners," he said, pulling out a crinkled twenty. "Here, this is for your trouble."

Austin stared down at the twenty.

Marc thrust the money at him. "Take it." There was an underlying threatening sound in his voice. The man's blue eyes were ice-cold.

"Please," Rebecca said. Austin still couldn't think of her as this man's wife. There was pleading in her voice, in her gaze.

"Thanks," he said as he took the money. "You really didn't have to, though."

Marc chuckled at that.

"Have a nice trip, then. Drive carefully." Austin turned and walked toward his rental SUV.

Behind him, he heard Marc say, "Get in the car."

When he turned back, she was pulling herself up into the large rig. He climbed into his own vehicle, but waited until the Suburban drove away. He caught only a glimpse of her wan face in the side window as they left. Her brown eyes were wide with more than tears. The woman seemed even more terrified.

His heart was already pounding like a war drum. That red mark around her right wrist. All his instincts told him that this was more than a bossy husband.

He tossed down the twenty and, reaching in his pocket, took out the scrap of paper she'd pressed into his palm. It appeared to be a corner of a page torn from a motel Bible. There were only four words, written in a hurried scrawl with an eyeliner pencil: "Help me. No law."

Chapter Seven

Austin looked down the main street where the black Suburban had gone. If Marc Stewart was headed for Helena, he was going the wrong way.

He hesitated only a moment before he started the engine, backed up and turned onto the street.

Bozeman was one of those Western towns that had continued to grow—unlike a lot of Montana towns. In part, its popularity was because of its vibrant and busy downtown as well as being the home of Montana State University.

Austin cursed the traffic that had him stopped at every light while the black Suburban kept getting farther away. What he couldn't understand was why Marc Stewart was headed southwest if he was anxious to get his wife home. Maybe they were going out for breakfast first.

He caught another stoplight and swore. The Suburban was way ahead and unfortunately a lot of people in Bozeman drove large rigs, which made it nearly impossible to keep the vehicle in sight. He was getting more nervous by the moment. All his instincts told him the woman hadn't been delusional. She was in trouble.

From the beginning, she'd said the car wasn't hers, the purse wasn't hers and that her name wasn't Rebecca Stewart. What if she had been telling the truth?

It was that thought that had him hitting the gas the moment the light changed. Determined not to have to stop at the next one, he sped through the yellow light and kept going. He sped through another yellow light, barely making it. But ahead, he could see the Suburban. It was headed southwest out of town.

That alone proved something, didn't it?

But what? That Marc Stewart had lied about wanting to get his wife home to Helena as quickly as possible. What else might he be lying about? The pregnancy?

Austin used the hands-free system in the SUV to put in a call to the doctor at the hospital who'd handled the case. He knew he couldn't ask outright about the patient's condition. But...

Dr. Mayfield came on the line.

"Doctor, it's Austin Cardwell. I'm the man who found Rebecca Stewart—"

"Yes, I remember you, Mr. Cardwell. What can I do for you?"

"I ended up with Mrs. Stewart's purse after last night's emergency." He was counting on the doctor not knowing he'd already stopped by the hospital earlier. "I wanted to drop it by if Mrs. Stewart is up to it."

"I'm sorry, but her husband checked her out earlier today."

"I noticed she has prenatal vitamins in her purse when I was looking for her identification."

A few beats of silence stretched out a little too long. "Mr. Cardwell, I'm not sure what Mrs. Stewart told you, but I'm not at liberty to discuss her condition."

"Understood." He'd heard the surprise in the silence before the doctor had spoken. "Oh, one more thing. I just wanted to be sure she got her watch before she left the hospital. She was worried about it."

"Just a moment." The doctor left the line. When he came back, he said, "Yes, her husband picked it up for her."

Her husband picked up the watch with the name Gillian on it?

"Thank you, Doctor." He disconnected. Ahead, he could see the black Suburban still headed west on Highway 191. Marc had lied about her being pregnant, but why?

Austin thought about calling Marshal Hud Savage, but what would he tell him? That Marc Stewart was a liar. That wasn't illegal. Even if he told the marshal about the note the woman had passed him or about the diamond watch with the wrong name on it, Austin doubted Hud would be able to do more than he already had. Not to mention Rebecca had specified, *No law.*

Her name isn't Rebecca, just as she'd said, he realized with a jolt.

It's Gillian. Gillian Cooper. Rebecca's sister? The thought hit him like a sledgehammer. That was the only thing she had reacted to last night other than the man who was pretending to be her husband. It was the name on the expensive watch. It was proof—

Austin groaned as he realized it proved nothing. If she was Rebecca, she could have a reason for wearing her sister's watch. He thought of a woman he knew who wore her brother's St. Christopher medal. Her brother had died of cancer a few years before.

So maybe there was no mystery to the watch. But the woman in that black Suburban was in trouble. She'd asked for his help. Even if she was Rebecca and Marc Stewart was her husband, she was terrified of him. Terrified enough to leave her child and run.

That was the part that just didn't add up. Maybe Marc

wouldn't let her take the child. All this speculation was giving him a headache.

Austin saw the four-way stop ahead. The black Suburban was in the left-hand turn lane. Marc Stewart was turning south—back up the Gallatin Canyon where Austin had found her the night before. So where was he going if not taking her home?

Instead of taking the highway south, though, the Suburban pulled into the gas station at the corner. Austin slowed, hanging back as far as he could as he saw Marc pull up to a gas pump and get out. The woman climbed out as well, said something to Marc and then went inside.

Austin saw his chance and pulled behind the station. He knew he didn't have much time since he wasn't sure why the woman had gone into the convenience store. If he was right, the man would be watching her, afraid to let her out of his sight. All he could hope was that the Suburban's gas tank was running low. He knew from experience that it took a long while to fill one.

Once inside the store, he looked around for the woman, anxious to find her since this might be his only chance to talk to her. There were several women in the store. None was the one he'd rescued last night.

It had only taken a few minutes for him to park. Surely she hadn't already gone back out to her vehicle. He glanced toward the Suburban from behind a tall rack of chips. Its front seats were both empty. Marc was still pumping gas into the tank, his gaze on the front of the store. The glare on the glass seemed to keep him from seeing inside. The woman was in here. Austin could think of only one other place she might be.

He found the restrooms down a short hallway. As she came out of the ladies' room, she saw him and froze.

Eyes wide with fear, she looked as if she might turn and run. Except there was nowhere to run. He was blocking her way out.

He rushed to her. "Talk to me. Tell me who you are and what is going on."

She shook her head, glancing past him as if terrified Marc Stewart would appear at any moment.

"You gave me the note. You obviously are in trouble. Let me help you."

"I'm sorry. I shouldn't have involved you," she said. "Please forget I did. You can't help me." She tried to step past him, but he grabbed her arm. She flinched.

"He hurt you again, didn't he?"

"You don't understand. He has my sister."

"Your *sister?*"

Tears welled in her eyes. "Rebecca. If I don't go with him—" Her eyes widened in alarm again and he realized a buzzer had announced that someone had entered the store. Fortunately he and the woman couldn't be seen where they were standing, though. At least not yet.

"Your name is Gillian, isn't it? The watch—"

"Where are your restrooms?" he heard Marc ask the clerk.

Gillian gripped his arm, her fingers digging into his flesh. "If you tell anyone, he'll kill her."

There wasn't time to reassure her. "Where's he taking you?"

"A cabin in Island Park."

"Here, take this. If you get a chance, call me." He pressed one of his business cards into her palm and then pushed into the men's restroom an instant before he heard Marc's voice outside the door.

"It took you long enough," Marc snapped. "Come on."

Austin waited until he was sure they were gone before

he opened the door and headed for his SUV. He had no idea what Island Park was or how to get there. All he knew was that he had no choice but to go after her.

Chapter Eight

As Gillian climbed into the Suburban, she could feel Marc watching her, his eyes narrowed.

"It took you long enough in there," he said, studying her. "You didn't try to make any calls while you were in there, did you?" he asked, his voice low. She knew how close he was to hitting her when his voice got like that.

"How would I have made a call? You have my cell phone, I have no money and, in case you haven't noticed, there aren't pay phones around anymore."

He narrowed his eyes in warning. She knew she was treading on thin ice with him, but kowtowing to him only seemed to make him more violent.

Marc was still staring at her as if searching for even a hint of a lie. "I figure if anyone could find a way, it would be you. I've learned the hard way what you're capable of, sister-in-law. Let's not forget that you've managed to get some local marshal sniffing around—not to mention a deputy from *Texas*."

"I told you that wasn't my doing. The deputy was merely worried about me." She looked away, wishing he would start the engine. He was looking for any excuse to hurt her again.

"*Worried about you?* That Texas cowboy took a shine to you after you told him you weren't my wife. You take a shine to him, too? The patrolman said the cowboy had you in some cabin handcuffed to a chair. He have his way with you?"

"You disgust me," she said and turned to look out the side window. A pickup had pulled up behind them, the driver now waiting for the gas pump.

"Gave you his coat. How gallant is that?" he said, his voice a sneer. "You must have done something to keep him coming back."

She wished he would just start the engine. "You know I didn't know what I was saying. I have a concussion. Or don't you believe that either?" She turned to face him, knowing it was a daring thing to do. He was just looking for an excuse. He hated everything about her and her sister.

"Right, your head injury from an accident that would never have happened if you hadn't—"

"Been running for my life?"

His face twisted into a mask of fury. "You—"

She braced herself for the smack she knew was coming. The only thing that saved her was the driver behind them honking loudly.

Marc swore and flipped the man off, but started the engine and pulled away from the pump and onto the highway headed south toward West Yellowstone.

Gillian breathed a small sigh of relief. All she'd done was buy herself a little time. She'd be lucky if Marc didn't kill her. Right now, she was more worried about what he'd already done to Rebecca.

"What are you looking at?" Marc snapped.

"Nothing," she said as she turned toward him.

"You were looking in your side mirror." He hurriedly checked his rearview. "Is that cowboy following us?"

She realized her mistake. "What cowboy?"

"Don't give me that what cowboy bull. You know damned well. That *Texas* cowboy. Did you see him back there?"

"In the ladies' room?" She scoffed at his paranoia. "I was only looking out the window." It was a lie and she feared he knew it.

He kept watching behind them as he drove. "If you said something to him back at the motel—"

"You were there. You know I didn't say anything. Why did you say Rebecca was pregnant with a baby girl?" She held her breath for his answer.

Marc let out a snort. "I figured it would just get the guy off my back once he thought you were pregnant." He chuckled as if pleased with himself and seemed to relax a little, although he kept watching his mirror.

She hated that she'd involved Austin Cardwell in all this, but she'd been so desperate... Now she prayed that if he really was following them, that he didn't let Marc see him. There was no telling what Marc would do.

"What did you tell him last night?"

Gillian didn't need to ask whom he was talking about. "I didn't even know who I was last night, so how was I going to tell him anything?"

"That was convenient. But you recognized *me* when you saw me, didn't you?"

She'd been so confused, so terrified and yet she hadn't known of what or whom. But once Marc had come into her hospital room, she'd remembered, even before he'd whispered in her ear, "I'll kill your sister if you don't go along with what I say."

It had all come back in a wave of misery that threatened to overwhelm her. When Marc had slipped her sister's wedding band onto her finger... She hadn't been able to hold back the tears. She'd made matching rings for her sister and Marc when they'd married. Marc had lost his almost at once, but Rebecca… She felt a sob try to work its way up out of her chest. If Marc was carrying Rebecca's wedding ring in his pocket, was she even still alive?

AUSTIN STAYED BACK, letting the black Suburban disappear down Highway 191 toward Big Sky, while he called Hud.

"I need a favor," he said. "Does Marc Stewart own a cabin in a place called Island Park?"

Silence, then, "I'm sure you have a good reason to ask."

"I do."

"Want to tell me what's going on?"

"I wish I could."

"I hope you know what you're doing," the marshal said.

Austin hoped so, as well.

More silence, then the steady clack of computer keys.

"Funny you should ask," Hud said when he came back on the line. "Marc Stewart has been paying taxes on a place in Island Park."

Austin leaned back, relieved, as he drove out of the valley and into the canyon. The traffic wasn't bad compared to Houston. Most every vehicle, other than semis, had a full ski rack on top. The roads had become more packed with snow, but at least he had some idea now where Marc Stewart might be heading.

"Where and what is Island Park?"

Hud rattled off an address that didn't sound like any he'd ever heard. "How do I find this place?" he asked frowning. "It doesn't sound like a street address in a town."

"Finding it could be tricky. Island Park is a thirty-three-mile-long town just over the Montana border from

West Yellowstone. Basically, it follows the highway. The so-called town is no more than five hundred feet wide in places. They call it the longest main street in the world."

"Seriously?"

Austin was used to tiny Texas towns or sprawling urban cities.

"Owners of the lodges along the highway incorporated back in 1947 to circumvent Idaho's liquor laws, which prohibited the sale of liquor outside city limits."

"So how do I find this cabin?"

"In the middle of winter? I'd suggest by snowmobile unless it is right off a plowed road, which will be doubtful. Have you ever driven a snowmobile?"

"No, but I'll manage." He'd deal with all that once he knew where to look for the cabin.

"I don't know Island Park at all so I can't help you beyond the address I gave you. I should warn you that you're really on your own once you cross the border into Idaho. I would imagine any help you might need from law enforcement would have to come out of Ashton, a good fifty miles to the south. Where you're headed is very isolated, with cabins back in heavily wooded areas. They get a lot of snow over there."

"Great." He'd already known that he was on his own. But now it was clear there would be no backup should he get himself in a bind. He almost laughed at that. He couldn't be in a worse situation right now, headed into country he didn't know and into a possible violent domestic dispute between Marc Stewart and his real wife.

"I suppose you won't be able to join us for dinner tonight?"

Austin had forgotten about dinner. "I'll try my best, but if things go south with this..."

"Not to worry. Dana is used to having a marshal for

a husband. Just watch your back. And keep in touch," Hud said.

Austin didn't see the black Suburban again on the drive through the canyon. When the road finally opened up, he found himself on what apparently was called Fir Ridge. Off to his left was a small cemetery in the aspens and pines. Then the highway dropped down into a wooded area before crossing the Madison River Bridge and entering the small tourist town of West Yellowstone.

Had Marc stopped here to get Gillian something to eat? Buy gas? Or was he just anxious to get to wherever he was going?

Austin had no way of knowing. He only knew that he couldn't cross paths with him if he hoped to keep Gillian alive. All his training told him to bring the law into this now. Going in like the Lone Ranger was always a bad idea—especially when you weren't sure what you were getting into.

And yet, he couldn't make himself do it. Gillian did not want the law involved. She was terrified of Marc Stewart, and with her sister in danger, Austin couldn't chance that calling in law enforcement would push Marc into killing not only her, but also her sister, as well.

Not that he wasn't worried about getting her killed himself. If only he'd had more time with Gillian at the convenience store. There was so much he needed to know. Such as where was Rebecca's young son, Andrew Marc? Was he really with his grandmother? Or was that, too, a lie?

West Yellowstone was a tourist town of gas stations, curio shops, motels and cafés. Austin took the first turn out and headed for the Idaho border. He still hadn't seen the black Suburban. He could only hope that Gillian was right about where Marc was taking her.

Last night, Gillian had been driving her sister's car. He suspected the registration, the purse, the baby car seat, even the suitcase in the back belonged to her sister, Rebecca.

From the way the clothes had been thrown into the suitcase, he was assuming Rebecca had tried to leave her husband. So how had Gillian ended up in her sister's car?

He had many more questions than he had answers. No wonder he felt anxious. Even if he hadn't been shot and almost died just months ago when a case had gone wrong, he would have been leery of walking into this mess. No law officer in his right mind wanted to go in blind.

His cell phone rang. He snatched it up with the crazy thought that somehow Gillian Cooper had gotten away from Marc and was now calling.

"Where the hell are you?" his brother Tag demanded. "You did remember that we're supposed to have dinner with Dana, didn't you?"

Austin swore under his breath. "Something has come up."

"*Something?* Like something came up and you couldn't make my wedding?"

"Do we have to go through this again? I'm sorry. If it wasn't important—"

"More important obviously than your family."

"Tag, I'll explain everything when I get back. I'm sure you can go ahead with…" He realized his brother had hung up on him.

NOT THAT HE could blame his brother. He disconnected, feeling like a heel. He had a bad habit of letting down the people he cared about. He blamed his job, but the truth was he felt more comfortable as a deputy than he did in any other relationship.

"Maybe I'm like my dad," he'd said to his mother when she'd asked him why of the five brothers, he was the one who was often at odds with the others. *"Look how great Dad is with his sons,"* he'd pointed out.

His parents had divorced years ago when Austin was still in diapers. His mother had taken her five boys to live in Texas while their father had stayed in Big Sky. Austin had hardly seen his father over the years. He knew that his brothers had now reconciled with him, but Austin didn't see that happening as far as he was concerned. He wouldn't be in Montana long enough, and the way things were going…

It amazed him that his mother always stood up for the man she'd divorced, the man who had fathered her boys. *"I won't have you talk about your father like that,"* his mother had said the last time they discussed it. *"Harlan and I did the best we could."*

Austin had softened his words. *"You did great, Mom. But let's face it, I could be more like Harlan Cardwell than even you want to admit."*

"Tell me, is there anything you care about, Austin?" she'd asked, looking disappointed in him.

"I care about my family, my friends, my town, my state."

"But not enough to make your own brother's wedding."

"I was on a case."

"And there was no one else who could handle it?"

"I needed to see it through. I might not be great at relationships, but I'm damned good at my job."

"Watch your language," she'd reprimanded. *"A job won't keep you warm at night, son. Someday you're going to realize that these relationships you treat so trivially*

*are more important than anything else in life. I thought
almost losing your life might have taught you something."*

As he dropped over the Idaho border headed for Island
Park, he thought no one would ever understand him since
he didn't even understand himself. He just knew that right
now Gillian Cooper needed him more than his brothers
or cousin Dana did. Just as the woman he'd tried to save
in Texas had needed him more than Tag had needed another attendant at his wedding.

He'd failed his family as well as that woman in Texas,
though, and it had almost cost him his life. He couldn't
fail this one.

"You look like hell."

Gillian didn't bother to react to Marc's snide comment as they drove into West Yellowstone. He wanted
to argue with her, to have an excuse to hit her. His anger
was palpable in the interior of the Suburban. She'd out-
witted him—at least for a while before she'd lost control
of Rebecca's car and crashed.

Her head ached and she felt sick to her stomach. How
much of it was from the accident? The doctor had discussed her staying another night, but Marc had told her
that her sister would be dead if she did. She wasn't sure
if her ailments were from her concussion solely or not.
She'd often felt sick to her stomach when she thought of
the man her sister had married.

"I'll get you something to eat," Marc said. "I don't
want you dying on me. At least not yet." He pulled into
a drive-through. "What do you want?"

She wasn't hungry, but she knew she needed to eat.
She would need all her strength once they reached the
cabin.

Marc didn't give her a chance to answer, though. "Give

us four burgers, a couple of large fries and two big colas."
As he dug his wallet out, she felt him looking at her.
"You're just lucky you didn't kill yourself last night. As
it is, you owe me for a car."

Just like Marc to make it about the money.

"I'm sure my insurance will pay for it," she said drily.
"If I get to make the claim."

He snorted as he pulled up to the next window and
paid. A few moments later, he handed her a large bag of
greasy smelling food.

Just the odor alone made her stomach turn. She
thought she might throw up. "I need to go to the bathroom." The business card Austin Cardwell had given her
was hidden in her jeans pocket. She knew she should have
thrown it away back at the convenience store, but Marc
hadn't given her a chance.

He shook his head. "You just went back at Four Cor-
ners."

"I have to go again." She had to get rid of the business
card. If Marc found it on her—

She regretted telling Austin where they were headed.
Not only had she put him in danger and possibly made
things even worse, but she wasn't sure he would be able
to find the cabin anyway. She'd stolen glances in the side
mirror and hadn't seen his SUV. He was a deputy sheriff
in Texas. What if he contacted law enforcement here?

No, she couldn't see him doing that. Just as she couldn't
see him giving up. He was back there somewhere. He'd
saved her life last night. But she wasn't so sure he could
pull it off again. Worse, she couldn't bear the thought that
she might get him killed.

If she could get to a phone, she could call the number on the card and plead with him not to get involved.
Even as she thought it, she knew he wouldn't be able to

turn back now. She'd seen how determined he was at the hospital and later at the motel room. Her heart went out to him. Why couldn't her sister have married someone like Austin Cardwell?

"You'll just have to hold it," Marc was saying. "Hand me one of the burgers and some fries," he said as he drove onto the highway again.

She dug in the bag and handed him a sandwich. The last thing she wanted was food, but she made herself gag down one of the burgers and a little of the cola. Marc ended up devouring everything else. She prayed her sister was still alive, but in truth she feared what was waiting for her at the cabin.

As they drove up over the mountain and dropped down into Idaho, she stared out the window at the tall banks of plowed snow on each side of the road. Island Park was famous for its snow—close to nine feet of it in an average winter. And where there was snow...

Three snowmobiles buzzed by like angry bees on the trail beside the highway and sped off, the colorful sleds catching the sunlight.

She stole a glance in the side mirror. The highway behind them was empty. Her stomach roiled at the thought that Austin was ahead of them because of their food stop, that he might be waiting at the cabin, not realizing just how dangerous Marc was.

Gillian closed her eyes, fighting tears. She'd been so afraid for her sister she'd been desperate when she'd asked for his help. If only she could undo what she'd done. The man had saved her life last night and this was how she repaid him, by getting him involved in this?

There was no saving any of them, she thought as more snowmobiles zoomed past, kicking up snow crystals into the bright blue winter sky. It wasn't until they passed a cabin with a brightly decorated tree in the front yard that she remembered with a start that Christmas was only a few days away.

Chapter Nine

Not long after the Idaho border, the terrain closed in with pines and more towering snowbanks. Austin started seeing snowmobilers everywhere he looked. They buzzed past on brightly colored machines, the drivers clad in heavy-duty cold-weather gear and helmets, which hid their faces behind the black plastic.

Even inside the SUV, he could hear the roar of the machines as they sped by—all going faster on the snow track next to him than he was on the snow-slick highway.

Just as Hud had told him, he began to see cabins stuck back in the pines. He would need directions. He figured he was also going to need a snowmobile, just as Hud had suggested, if the cabin was far off the road.

When he reached the Henry's Fork of the Snake River, he pulled into a place alongside the highway called Pond's Lodge. The temperature seemed to be dropping, and tiny snowflakes hung around him as if suspended in the air as he got out of the SUV. He shivered, amazed that people lived this far north.

Inside, he asked for a map of the area.

"You'll want a snowmobile map, too," the older woman behind the counter said.

He thought she might be right as he stepped back outside. Snow had begun falling in huge lacy flakes. He wasn't all that anxious to get out in it on a snowmobile for the first time. But after a quick perusal of the map, he knew a snowmobile was his best bet.

As the marshal had told him he would, he could see the problem of finding the cabin—especially in winter. He figured a lot of the dwellings would be boarded up this time of year. Some even inaccessible.

He had to assume that Marc Stewart's family cabin would be open—but possibly not the road to it. What few actual roads there were seemed to be banked in deep snow. Clearly most everyone traveled by snowmobile. He could hear them buzzing around among the trees in a haze of gray smoke.

Back in his rented SUV, he drove down to a small out-of-the-way snowmobile rental. The moment he walked in the door, he caught the scent of a two-stroke engine and the high whine of several others as two snowmobiles roared out of the back of the shop. Even the music playing loudly from overhead speakers behind the counter couldn't drown them out. Beneath the speakers, a man in his late twenties with dozens of tattoos and piercings glanced up. The name stitched on his shirt read "Awesome."

"My man!" he called. "Looking for the ultimate machine, right? Are we talking steep and deep action or outrageous hill banging to do some high marking today?"

The man could have been speaking Greek. "Sorry, I just need one that runs."

Awesome laughed. "If it's boondocking you're looking for, chutes, ridges, big bowls, I got just the baby for you." He shoved a map at him. "We have an endless supply of cornices to jump, untouched powder and more coming down, mountainsides just waiting for you to put some fresh tracks on them."

"Do you have one for flat ground?"

Awesome looked a little disappointed. "You seriously want to pass up Two Top, Mount Jefferson and Lion's Head?"

He seriously did. "I see on your brochure that you have GPS tours. It says here I can pinpoint an area I want to go to with the specific coordinates and you can get me there?"

"I can." Awesome didn't seem all that enthusiastic about it, though. "We have about a thousand miles of backwoods trails."

"Great. Here is where I need to go. You have a machine that can get me there?"

He looked at the map, his enthusiasm waning even faster. "This address isn't far from here. I suppose you need gear? Helmet, boots, bibs, coat and gloves? They're an extra twenty. I can put you in a machine that will run you a hundred a day."

"How fast do these things go," Austin asked as one sped by in a blur.

"The fastest? A hundred and sixty miles an hour. The ones we have? You can clock in at a hundred."

Austin had no desire to clock in at a hundred. Even the price tag shocked him. The one sitting on the showroom floor was on sale for fourteen thousand dollars and everyone around here seemed to have one. He figured Marc Stewart would have at least one of the fastest snowmobiles around. He tagged the guy as someone who had done his share of high marking. "What is high marking, by the way?"

Awesome laughed and pointed at a poster on the wall. "You try to make the highest mark on the side of a mountain." On the poster, the rider had made it all the way up under an overhanging wall of snow."

"It looks dangerous."

Awesome shrugged. "Only if you get caught in an avalanche."

Austin didn't have to worry about avalanches, but what he was doing was definitely dangerous. Gillian was terrified for her sister. Austin wouldn't be trying to find them if he didn't believe she had good reason for concern.

But he was smart enough to know that a man like Marc Stewart, when trapped, might do something stupid like kill an off-duty state deputy sheriff who was sticking his nose where it didn't belong.

GILLIAN LOOKED OUT through the snow-filled pines as Marc drove. She couldn't see the cabin from the road. She'd been here once before, but it had been in summer. The cabin sat on Island Park Reservoir just off Centennial Loop Trail. While old, it was charming and picturesque. At least that's what she'd thought that summer she and her sister had spent a week here without Marc.

That had been before Rebecca and Marc had married, back when her sister had been happy and foolishly naive about the man she'd fallen in love with.

Gillian hugged herself as she remembered her sister's text message just days before.

On way to your house. I've left Marc.

She'd tried her sister's number, but the call went straight to voice mail. She'd texted back. Are you and Andy all right?

No answer. Helena was a good two hours away from Gillian's home in Big Sky. Even the way her sister drove, Rebecca wouldn't have arrived until after dark. Gillian had paced, checking the window anxiously and asking herself, "What would Marc do?" She feared the answer.

It was night by the time she finally saw her sister's

car pull up out front. Relieved to tears, she'd run out-side without even a coat on. But it hadn't been Rebecca in the car.

By the time she'd realized it was Marc alone and fu-rious, it was too late. He'd grabbed her and thrown her into the trunk. She'd fought him, but he'd been so much stronger and he'd taken her by surprise. He'd slammed the trunk lid and the next thing she'd known the car was moving.

"Did you really forget your name?" Marc asked, drag-ging her out of her thoughts. He sounded amused at the idea. "Sometimes I'd like to forget my name. Hell, I'd like to forget my life."

She didn't tell him that pieces of memory had her even more confused. She'd remembered there was someone in the trunk of the car she'd been driving, but she hadn't remembered it was her.

When Austin had returned to the cabin with the pa-trolman, he'd told her that the only thing he'd found in the trunk of the car was a suitcase. She'd been more confused.

It wasn't until she'd laid eyes on her alleged *husband* that she'd remembered Marc forcing her into the trunk. When he'd stopped at a convenience mart in the canyon, she'd shoved her way out by kicking aside the backseat.

She hadn't known where they were when she'd crawled out. He'd left the car running because of the freezing cold night. Not knowing where she was, she'd just taken off driving, afraid that he would get a ride or steal a car and come after her.

The next thing she remembered was waking up in a hospital with vague memories of the night before and a tall Texas cowboy.

"I'm curious. Where was it you thought you were

going?" Marc asked. He sounded casual enough, but she could hear the underlying fury behind his words.

"I have no idea." She'd been running scared. All she'd been able to think about was getting to a phone so she could call the police. Her cell phone had been in her pocket when she'd rushed out of her house, but Marc had taken it.

"You should have waited and run me down with the car." Marc glanced over at her. "Short of killing me, you should have known you wouldn't get away."

She shuddered at the thought, but knew he was right. She had managed to get away from him, but not long enough to help herself or her sister. Maybe that had been a godsend. He'd told her at the hospital that if they didn't get back to her sister soon, she would be dead.

Gillian hadn't known then where he'd left Rebecca. But she'd believed him. He'd had her sister's wedding band in his pocket. It wasn't until Marc headed out of Bozeman that she'd figured out where he was taking her.

Now Marc slowed the Suburban as he turned down a narrow road with high snowbanks on each side. He drove only a short distance, though, before the road ended in a huge pile of snow. She glanced around as he pulled into a wide spot where the snow had been plowed to make a parking area. Other vehicles were parked there, most of them with snowmobile trailers.

"Here." He tossed her a pair of gloves. A snowmobile buzzed past, kicking up a cloud of snow. "If you want to see your sister alive, you will do what I say. Try to make another run for it—"

"I get it." As angry and out of control as he was, she feared what kind of shape her sister was in. Marc had told Austin that their son, Andrew Marc, was with his grandmother. That had been a lie since Marc's parents were both dead and he had no other family that she knew of.

So where was Andy? Was he with his mother at the cabin? She didn't dare hope that they were both safe.

Marc backed up to where he'd left his snowmobile trailer. Both machines were on it, Gillian noticed, and any hope she'd had that her sister might have escaped evaporated at the sight of them. Even if Rebecca was able to leave the cabin, she had no way to get out. The snow would be too deep. One step off the snowmobile and she would be up to her thigh in snow. As she glanced in the direction of the cabin, Gillian could see the fresh tracks that Marc had made in and back out again from the cabin on the deep snow. Neither trip had packed down the trail enough to walk on.

Marc cut the engine. She could hear the whine of snowmobiles in the distance, then an eerie quiet fell over the Suburban.

"Come on," he said as he reached behind the seat for his coat. "Your sister is waiting."

Was she? Gillian could only pray it was true as she pulled on the coat Austin had given her and climbed out into the falling snow. Even as she breathed in the frosty air, she prayed they hadn't arrived too late. Marc had told her last night that if Rebecca was dead, it was her fault for taking off in the car and causing him even more problems.

The only thing that made her climb onto the back of the snowmobile behind her brother-in-law was the thought of her sister and nephew. Whatever was going on, Marc had brought her here for a reason. She couldn't imagine what. But if she could save Rebecca and Andy...

Even as she thought it, Gillian wondered how she would do that against a man like Marc Stewart.

AUSTIN WAS PLEASED to find that driving a snowmobile wasn't much different from driving a dirt bike. Actually, it was easier because you didn't have to worry as much about balance. You could just sit down, hit the throttle and go.

With the GPS in his pocket, along with a map of the area, and his weapon strapped on beneath his coat, he headed for Marc Stewart's cabin. The area was a web of narrow snow-filled roads that wove through the dense pines. From what he could gather, the Stewart cabin was on the reservoir.

He followed Box Canyon Trail until it connected with another trail at Elk Creek. Then he took Centennial Loop Trail.

He passed trees with names on boards tacked to them. Dozens of names indicating dozens of cabins back in the woods. But he had a feeling that the Stewart cabin wasn't near a lot of others or at least not near an occupied cabin.

Snowmobiles sped past, throwing up new snow, leaving behind blue exhaust. It was snowing harder by the time he reached the spot on the GPS where he was supposed to turn.

He slowed. The tree next to the road had only four signs nailed on it. Three of them were Stewart's. Off to his right, Austin saw a half dozen vehicles parked at what appeared to be the entrance to another trailhead that went off in the opposite direction from the Stewart family cabins.

The black Suburban was parked in front of a snowmobile trailer with one machine on it. There were fresh snow tracks around the spot where a second one must have recently been unloaded.

Austin double-checked the GPS. It appeared the cabin

at the address the marshal had given him was a half mile down a narrow road.

As he turned toward the road, he saw that there were several sets of snowmobile tracks, but only one in the new snow—and it wasn't very old based on how little of the falling snow had filled it.

Marc and Gillian weren't that far ahead of him.

Chapter Ten

The road Austin had taken this far was packed down from vehicles driving on it. But the one that went back into the cabins hadn't been plowed since winter had begun so the snow was a good five or six feet deep.

Austin had to get a run at it, throttling up the snowmobile to barrel up the slope onto the snow.

Fortunately, the snowmobile ahead of him had packed down the new snow so once he got up on top of it, the track was fairly smooth. Still, visibility was bad with the falling snow and the dense trees. He couldn't see anything ahead but the track he was on. According to the map, the road went past the Stewart cabins for another quarter mile before it ended beside the lake.

His plan was to go past the cabin where the snowmobile had gone, then work his way back. As loud as the snowmobile motor was, it would be heard by anyone inside the cabin. His only hope for a surprise visit would be if those inside thought he was merely some snowmobiler riding around.

A corner of a log cabin suddenly appeared from out of the falling snow. Austin caught glimpses of more weathered dark log structures as he continued on past. The shingled roofs seemed to squat under the layers of snow, the smaller cabins practically disappearing in the drifts.

No smoke curled out of any of the rock chimneys. In fact as he passed, he saw no signs of life at all. Wooden shutters covered all the windows. No light came from within.

He would have thought that the cabins were empty, still closed up waiting for spring—if not for the distinct new snowmobile track that cut off from the road he was on and headed directly for the larger of the three cabins.

Austin kept the throttle down, the whine of his snow-mobile cutting through the cold silence of the forest as he zoomed past the cabins huddled in the pines and snow. He stole only a couple of glances, trying hard not to look in their direction for fear of who might be looking back.

MARC PULLED AROUND the back of the cabin and shut off the snowmobile engine.

Gillian could barely hear over the thunder of her heart. Her legs felt weak as she slipped off the back of the machine and looked toward the door of the cabin. The place was big and rambling, dated in a way that she'd found quaint the first time her sister had invited her here.

"Isn't this place something?" Rebecca had said, clearly proud of what she called Stewart Hall.

The main cabin reminded Gillian of the summer lodges she'd seen on television. All of it told of another time: the log and antler decor, furniture with Western print fabric, the bookshelves filled with thick tomes and board games, and the wide screened-in front porch with its wicker rockers that looked out over a marble-smooth green lake surrounded by towering pines.

"It is picturesque," Gillian had said, not mentioning that it smelled a little musty. *"How often does Marc's family get up here?"*

"There isn't much family left. Just Marc and me."

Rebecca's hand had gone to her stomach. Her eyes brightened. *"That's why he wanted to start our family as soon as possible."*

"You're pregnant?*"* Her sister and Marc had only been married a few months at that time. But Gillian had seen how happy her sister was. *"Congratulations,"* she'd said and hugged Rebecca tightly as she remembered how she'd tried to talk her out of marrying Marc and her sister had accused her of being jealous.

Now as she watched Marc pocket the snowmobile key, she wished she'd fought harder. Even when they were only dating, Gillian had seen a selfishness in Marc, a need to always be the center of attention, a need to have everything his way. He was a poor sport, too, often leaving games in anger. They'd been small things that Rebecca had ignored, saying no man was perfect.

Gillian wished she had fought harder. Maybe she could have saved Rebecca from a lot of pain. But then there would be no baby. No little Andy...

"You know what you have to do," Marc said as he reached in another pocket for the key to the door.

She nodded.

"Do I have to remind you what happens if you don't?" he asked.

Gillian looked into his eyes. It was like looking into the fires of hell. "No," she said. "You were quite clear back at the motel."

AUSTIN RODE FARTHER up the road until he could see another cabin in the distance. He found a spot to turn the snowmobile around. The one thing he hadn't considered was how hard it would be to hike back to the Stewart cabins.

The moment he stepped off the machine, his leg sunk

to his thighs in the soft snow. His only hope was to walk in the snowmobile track—not that he didn't sink a good foot with each step.

He checked his gun and extra ammunition and then headed down the track. The falling snow made him feel as if he were in a snow globe. Had he not been following the snowmobile track, he might have become disoriented and gotten lost in what seemed an endless forest of snow-covered trees that all looked the same.

An eerie quiet had fallen around him, broken only by the sound of his own breathing. He was breathing harder than he should have been he realized. It had been months now since he'd been shot. That had been down on the Mexico border with heat and cactus and the scent of dust in the air, nothing like this. And yet, he had that same feeling that he was walking into something he wouldn't be walking back out of—and all because of a woman.

A bird suddenly cried out from a nearby tree. Austin started. He couldn't remember ever feeling more alone. When he finally picked up the irritating buzz of snowmobiles in the distance, he was thankful for a reminder of other life. The snow had an insulating effect that rattled his nerves with its cold silence. That and the memory of lying in the Texas dust, dying.

It seemed he'd been wrong. He hadn't put it behind him, he realized with a self-deprecating chuckle. And now here he was again. Only this time, he didn't know the area, let alone what was waiting for him inside that cabin, and he wasn't even a deputy doing his job.

The structure appeared out of the falling snow. He realized he couldn't stay on the track. But when he stepped off into the deep snow, he found himself laboring to move. It was worse under the trees, where it formed deep wells. If you got too close… He stepped into one and dropped, finding himself instantly buried. He fought his way to the surface like a swimmer and finally was able to climb out. The snow had chilled him. He'd never been in snow, let alone anything this deep and cold.

But his biggest concern was what awaited him ahead. He had no idea what he was going to do when he reached the main cabin. He needed to know what was going on inside. Unfortunately, with the shutters on all the windows, he wasn't sure how to accomplish that.

As he neared the side, he saw an old wooden ladder hanging on an outbuilding and had an idea. It was a crazy one, but any idea seemed good right now. The snow was deep enough where it had drifted in on this side of the cabin that it ran from the roof to the ground. If he could lay the ladder against the snowdrift, it was possible he could climb up onto the roof. The chimney stuck up out of the snow only a few feet. With luck, he might be able to hear something.

The snowmobile that had made the recent tracks to the cabin was parked out back—just as he'd suspected. Steam was still coming off the engine, indicating that whoever had ridden it hadn't been at the cabin long.

Austin took the ladder and, working his way through the snow, leaned it against the house and began to climb.

It was like a tomb inside the cabin with the shutters closed and no lights or heat on. Gillian stood in the large living room waiting for Marc to turn on a lamp. When he did, she blinked, blinded for a moment.

In that instant, she saw the cabin the way it had been the first time she'd seen it. The Native American rugs, the pottery and the old paintings and photographs on the walls. The vintage furniture and the gleam of the wood floors.

She'd felt back then that she'd been transported to another time, one that felt grander. One she wished she'd had as a child. She'd envied Marc his childhood here on this lake. How she'd longed to have been the little girl who curled up in the hammock out on the porch and read books on a long, hot summer day while her little sister played with dolls kept in one of the old trunks.

If only they could have been two little girls who swam in the lake and learned to water-ski behind the boat with her two loving parents. And lay in bed at night listening to the adults, the lodge alive with laughter and summer people.

For just an instant, Gillian had heard the happy clink of crystal from that other time. Then Marc stepped on a piece of broken glass that splintered under his snowmobile boot with the sound of a shot. He kicked it away and Gillian saw the room how it was now, cold, dark and as broken as the lonely only child Marc Stewart had been.

Most of the lighter-weight furniture now looked like kindling. Anything that could be broken was. Jigsaw pieces of ceramic vases, lamps and knickknacks littered the floor, along with the glass from the picture frames.

The room attested to the extent of Marc Stewart's rage—not that Gillian needed a reminder.

She looked toward the large old farmhouse-style kitchen. The floor was deep in broken dishes and thrown cutlery.

Past it down the hall, she saw drops of blood on the worn wood floor.

"Where's my sister? Rebecca!" Her voice came out too high. It sounded weak and scared and without hope. *"Rebecca?"*

"She's not up here," Marc said as he kicked aside what was left of a spindle rocking chair.

The weight of the fear on her chest made it hard to even say the words. *"Where is she?"*

"Down there." He pointed toward the old root cellar door off the kitchen.

Gillian felt her heart drop like a stone. She couldn't get her legs to move. Just as she couldn't get her lungs to fill. "You left her down there all this time?"

"We would have been here sooner if it wasn't for you." Marc looked as if he wanted to hit her, as if it took everything in him not to break her as he had everything else in this cabin. "Are you coming?"

AUSTIN CLIMBED ACROSS the roof to the chimney. The snow silenced his footfalls, but also threatened to slide in an avalanche that would take him with it should he misstep. He knelt next to the chimney to listen just as he heard Gillian call out her sister's name.

He waited for an answer.

He heard none.

"Can't you bring her up here?" Austin heard the fear in Gillian's voice. Bring her up? Was there a basement under the cabin? He didn't think so. A root cellar possibly? Then he felt his skin crawl as he remembered a root cellar one of his friends had found at an old abandoned house. He was instantly reminded of the musky smell, the cobwebs, the dust-coated canning jars with unidentifiable contents and the scurry of the rats as they'd opened the door.

"I thought you understood that we were doing this my way," Marc said, his tone as threatening as the smack that followed his words and Gillian's small cry of pain. "Come on."

Austin heard what sounded like the crunch of boot heels over gravel, then nothing for a few moments.

Chapter Eleven

Gillian peered down the steep wooden stairs into the dim darkness and felt her stomach roil. Only one small light burned in a black corner of the root cellar. The musty, damp smell hit her first.

"Rebecca?" she called and felt Marc shove her hard between her shoulder blades. She would have tumbled headlong down the stairs if she hadn't grabbed the door frame.

"Move," Marc snapped behind her.

Gillian thought she heard a muffled sound down in the blackness, but it could have been pack rats. What if Marc had lied? What if Rebecca was dead? Then the only reason Marc had come after her and brought her back here was to kill her, too.

She took one step, then another. There was no railing so she clung to the rough rock wall that ran down one side of the stairs. With each step, she expected Marc to push her again. All her instincts told her this was a trap. She wouldn't have been surprised to hear him slam and lock the door at the top of the steps behind her. Leaving her to die down here would be the kind of cruel thing he would do.

To her surprise, she heard the steps behind her groan with his weight as he followed her down. It gave her little relief, though. The moment she reached the bottom, she turned on him. "Where is she? Marc, where is my sister?"

Gillian heard another moan and turned in the direction the sound had come from. Something moved deep in the darkest part of the root cellar. "Oh, God, what have you done to her?"

Marc pushed her aside. An instant later, a bare overhead bulb turned on blinding her. Gillian blinked, shielding her eyes from the glare as she tried to see—all the time terrified of what Marc had done to her sister.

In the far reaches of the root cellar, Gillian saw her. Rebecca was shackled to a chair. He'd left her water and a bucket along with at least a little food. But there was dried blood on her face and clothes. Her face was also bruised and raw, but her eyes were open.

What Gillian saw in her sister's eyes, though, sent her heart plummeting. Regret when she saw her sister, but when her gaze turned to her husband, it was nothing but defiance. Gillian tried to swallow, but her mouth felt as if filled with cotton balls.

"You're her last hope, big sister," Marc said as he looked from his wife to her. "Get her to tell you what she did with my ledger, my money and my son…" He met her gaze. "Or I will kill her and then I will beat it out of you since I know she tells you everything."

Not everything, Gillian thought. She swallowed again, her throat working. "I already told you that I don't know."

He nodded, his facial features distorted under the harsh glare of the single bulb hanging over his head. How could such a handsome man look so evil…?

"Either you get it out of her or I will beat her until her last scream." He handed her a key to the lock on the shackles.

Gillian moved to her sister, falling on her knees in

front of her. She worked to free her, her hands shaking so hard she had trouble with the lock. "She needs water and food and help out of this chair." She turned to glare back at him. "It's too cold and damp down here. I think she is already suffering from hypothermia. She's going to die before you can kill her."

He took a step toward her. "Who the hell do you think you are, telling me what I *have* to do?"

It took all of her courage to stand up to him knowing the kind of man he was. But if she and Rebecca had any chance, they had to get out of this root cellar.

"If she dies, then what she knows dies with her," Gillian said quickly. "I told you. I don't know. She didn't tell me because she knows I'm not as strong as she is. I would tell you."

He seemed to mull that over for a moment, his gaze going to his wife. Marc looked livid. He raised his hand and Gillian tried not to cower from his fist.

To her surprise, he didn't strike her. "Fine," he said with a curse.

Rebecca didn't move, didn't seem to breathe. If it weren't for the movement of her eyes, Gillian would have sworn she was already dead.

"I hope you don't think you're going to get away again," Marc said, meeting her gaze. "I have nothing to lose and I'm sick of both of you."

Austin heard the sound of footfalls and murmured voices. He froze, listening, and was relieved when he heard Gillian's voice. He hadn't been able to hear anything for a while.

"We need to get her warm." Her voice was louder. So were the footfalls. They'd come up from the root cellar.

He also heard another sound, a slow shuffling, almost dragging, gait.

"Maybe you could build a fire or turn on the furnace."

Marc swore at Gillian's suggestion. The footfalls stopped abruptly. Gillian let out a small cry. Austin cringed in anger, knowing that Marc had hit her.

"Enough wasting time," Marc snapped.

"You want her to talk? Then give me a chance. But first we need to warm her up. Can you get some quilts from the bedroom?"

Marc swore loudly, but Austin heard what sounded like him storming away into another room. "Move and I'll—" he said over his shoulder.

"I'm not going to move," Gillian snapped. "My sister can barely stand, let alone run away. I'm going to put her in the living room in front of the fireplace. Maybe you could build a fire?"

Austin didn't catch what Marc said. He could guess, though. Marc was an abusive SOB. But Austin still had no idea why he'd brought Gillian and her sister here, nor where the child was. From what he had surmised, Marc thought Gillian could get her sister to talk, but talk about what?

Austin decided it didn't matter. Marc had forced Gillian to come here against her will. He had abused her and her sister and had apparently held Rebecca captive here. It was time to put a stop to this.

Working his way back off the roof, he walked around to where Marc had left the snowmobile. All Austin's instincts warned him not to go busting in. He couldn't chance what Marc would do.

He moved carefully back the way he'd come until he was at the far side of the cabin complex. He found an old door with a single lock and waited until he heard the sound of several snowmobiles nearby. Hoping they would drown out the noise, he busted the lock and carefully shoved open the door.

GILLIAN HELPED HER SISTER into a straight-backed chair from the dining room and gently wiped her sister's face with the hem of her sweater. "Oh, Becky."

Rebecca's gaze locked with hers, her voice a hoarse whisper. "I thought I could do this without getting you involved."

Marc returned with the quilts and dropped them next to the chair.

"We're going to need a fire," Gillian said, not looking at him as she rubbed life back into her sister's hands and arms.

After a moment, she glanced over her shoulder to see what Marc was doing. He was busy building a fire in the rock fireplace using some of the furniture he'd destroyed. He struck a match to the wadded up newspaper under the stack of wood. The paper caught fire. The dried old wood of the furniture burst into flames and began to crackle warmly.

"She needs something to drink. Is there any water in the kitchen?"

"What do you think?" Marc snapped. "It's winter. Everything is shut off."

"Maybe you could melt some snow." She motioned with her head for him to go as if the two of them were in collaboration. The thought made her sick.

He glanced from her to her sister and back again. "Don't do anything stupid," he said as he walked into the kitchen and came back out with a pot in one hand.

Marc had both women in an old cabin in the woods, far enough from the rest of the world that they would never be found if he killed them and buried them in the root cellar. So what was the stupid thing he thought she might do?

He gave her a warning look anyway and left, going out the back door where he'd left the snowmobile. She let go of her sister's arms and to her surprise Rebecca fell over in the chair, catching herself before she fell on the littered floor.

Gillian helped her sit up straighter, shocked at how weak her sister was and terrified she wasn't going to survive this.

Marc came back in, shot them a look, but said nothing as he headed for the kitchen with the cooking pot full of fresh snow. She heard him turn on the stove. She could feel time slipping through her fingers.

"Becky, what's going on?" she whispered. "What is this about some ledger of Marc's? And where is Andy?"

Her sister shook her head in answer as she glanced toward the kitchen, where Marc was cussing and banging around.

"Tell him what he wants to know—otherwise he is going to kill you," Gillian pleaded.

"So sorry to get you—" her sister said from between cracked and cut lips.

"Becky—"

"Remember when we were kids and that big old tree blew over?"

Gillian stared at her. Had her brain been injured as a result of Marc's beating? Gillian's heartbreak rose in a sob from her throat as she looked at what that bastard had done to her sister.

Rebecca suddenly gripped her arm, digging in her fingernails. "Tell me you remember," her sister said.

"I remember."

Her sister's eyes filled with tears. "Love you." She licked her lips, her words coming out hoarse and hurried. "Save Andy. Make Marc pay." Pain filled her sister's eyes. "Can't save me."

"Stop talking like that. I'm not leaving here without you."

Her sister smiled, even though her lips were cut and bleeding, and then shook her head. "Get away. Run. He'll hurt you." She stopped talking at the sound of heavy footfalls headed back in their direction.

Gillian stared at her sister. "What are you going to do?" she whispered frantically. She could feel Marc closing the distance.

"Get ready to run," her sister said under her breath as Marc's shadow fell over them.

"What's all the whispering about?" Marc demanded as he handed Gillian a cup of melted snow.

She held it up to her sister's swollen lips. Her gaze met Rebecca's in a pleading gesture. Her sister was talking crazy. Worse, she seemed about to do something that could get them both killed.

Without warning, her sister knocked the cup out of her hand. It hit the floor, spilling the water as it rolled across the floor.

"You stupid—" Marc shoved Gillian out of the way. She fell backward and hit the floor hard. From where she was sprawled, she saw him pull his gun and crouch down in front of Rebecca. He put the end of the barrel against his wife's forehead. "Last chance, Rebecca."

With horror, Gillian saw Becky's expression—and what she had picked up from the floor and hidden in her hand. "No!" she screamed as her sister swung her arm toward Marc's face. The shard of sharp broken glass clutched in her fingers momentarily flashed as it caught the dim light.

Blood sprouted across Marc's cheek and neck as Rebecca raked the glass down his face. He bucked back and then shoved the barrel of the gun toward Rebecca's head as Gillian scrambled to her feet and launched herself at him.

The sound of the gunshot boomed, drowning out Gillian's scream as she careened into him, knocking them both to the floor.

THE DOORKNOB TURNED in Austin's hand as he heard the scream. He charged into the cabin, running toward the echoing sound of the scream and the gunshot, his heart hammering in his chest.

His lungs ached with the freezing-cold musty smell of the cabin. He had his gun drawn, his senses on alert, as he burst into the room and tried to take in everything at once. He saw it all in those few crucial seconds. The large wrecked living room; the small glowing fire crackling in the huge stone fireplace; snowy, melting footprints on the worn wood floor; and three people—all on the floor.

"Drop the gun!" Austin ordered as he saw Gillian and Marc struggling for the weapon. The other figure—Rebecca Stewart, he assumed—lay in a pool of blood next to them.

There was no way he could get a clear shot. He rushed forward an instant before the sound of the second gunshot ripped through the room. The bullet whistled past him. Marc wrestled the gun from Gillian and scrambled to his feet, dragging her up with him as a shield, the barrel of his gun against her temple.

"You drop *your* gun or so help me I will put a bullet

in her head," Marc said, sounding in pain. Austin saw that he was bleeding from a cut down his cheek and neck.

"You can't get away," Austin said his weapon aimed at Marc's head.

Marc chuckled at that as he lifted Gillian off her feet and backed toward the door where he'd left his snowmobile. "Drop your gun or I swear I will kill her!" Marc bellowed. His eyes were wide, blood streaming down his face, but the gun in his hand was steady and sure.

"The police are on their way. Let her go!" Austin doubted the bluff would work and it was too risky to try a shot since Marc was making himself as small a target as possible behind Gillian.

Marc kept backing toward the door. His snowmobile was just outside. If he could manage to get to it... Austin couldn't stand the thought of the man getting away, but his first priority had to be the safety of the women. Austin knew Marc wouldn't try to take Gillian with him. He needed to get away quickly. If he could make him let her go... He wouldn't be surprised, though, if at the last moment Marc put a bullet in her head.

Gillian was crying, the look on her face one of horror more than terror. She was looking at her sister crumpled on the floor in front of the fireplace. Rebecca wasn't moving.

Marc dragged Gillian another step back. He would have to let Gillian go to open the door. Austin waited as the seconds ticked by.

As Marc reached behind him to open the door, Austin knew he would have only an instant to take his shot. Moving fast, Marc shoved Gillian away, turned the gun and fired as Austin dove to the side for cover—and took his own shot.

He heard a howl of pain and then a loud crash, looking

in time to see Marc grab a large old wooden hutch by the door and pull it down after him. The hutch crashed down on its side, blocking the door as Marc made his escape.

Austin raced toward the door but couldn't see Marc or the snowmobile to get off a shot. As he started to scramble over the downed hutch, he heard the engine, smelled the smoke as the man roared away.

Behind him, Gillian, sobbing hysterically, pushed herself up from the littered floor and rushed to her sister.

His need to go after Marc blinded him for a moment. He'd wounded Marc, but it hadn't been enough to stop him. He couldn't bear the thought of Marc getting away after what he'd done. He swore under his breath. But as badly as he wanted the man, he couldn't leave Gillian and her sister to chase after him.

"Help her," she pleaded from where she was kneeling on the floor. "My sister—"

He holstered his gun and knelt down next to Rebecca to feel for a pulse. "She's alive." Just barely. He checked his phone. Still no service.

"Go for help. I'll stay here with her," Gillian said. "Go."

Chapter Twelve

Marc couldn't believe this. He was bleeding like a stuck pig. Reaching the road and his Suburban, he stumbled off the snowmobile and lurched toward his vehicle. He couldn't tell how badly he was wounded, but his movements felt too slow, which he figured indicated that he was losing blood fast.

He thumbed the key fob, opened the Suburban's door and pulled himself inside. The last thing he wanted to do was take the time to check his wounds for fear the cowboy would be coming after him, but something told him if he didn't stop the bleeding, he was a dead man either way.

The Texas deputy had said he'd already called the cops. Marc couldn't risk that the man was telling the truth. His hand shook as he turned the rearview mirror toward him and first inspected the cut.

"Son of a bitch!" He couldn't believe what Rebecca had done to him. The cut ran from just under his eye, down his cheek to under his chin and into his throat. He took off his gloves and pressed one to the spot that seemed to be bleeding the most.

After a few moments, the bleeding slowed—at least on his face. He could feel blood running down his side, chilling him as it soaked into his clothing. He became aware of the pain. His shoulder felt as if it were on fire. Unzipping his coat, then unbuttoning his shirt, he inspected the damage.

Again, he'd been lucky. The bullet had only grazed his shoulder. He stuck the other glove on the wound and zipped his coat back up. He would have to get more clothes. He couldn't wear a coat drenched in blood with a bullet hole in it—especially given the way his face looked.

He swore again, furious with Rebecca but even more furious with himself. She'd purposely pushed him so he would pull the trigger. Now he was no closer to finding his ledger and his money—or his son—than he had been at first.

Starting the Suburban, he pulled away. He would have to ditch this rig and pick up another. That was the least of his problems. He knew someone who could stitch up his wounds and get him another vehicle.

But now he was a man on the run from the law.

GILLIAN WAS CRADLING her sister's head in her arms when Austin returned with local law enforcement. Rebecca was breathing, but she hadn't regained consciousness. Gillian had wanted to go in the ambulance with her sister, but the officer had needed her to answer questions about what had happened.

"I'll take you to the Bozeman hospital to see your sister," Austin said when the interrogation had finally ended and they were allowed to go.

Gillian was still shaken and worried about her sister as she climbed into Austin's SUV. The officers who'd questioned them had taken them to a local station to talk. She'd been grateful to get out of the cold cabin.

"We have to make sure Marc doesn't get to Becky," she said as Austin pulled onto Highway 191, headed north.

"That isn't going to happen. There will be a guard out-side her room at the hospital, not that I suspect Marc will try to see her. There is a BOLO out on your brother-in-law. He can't get far in that large black Suburban. Also, he's wounded and needs medical attention. Law enforce-ment has thrown a net over the area. When he shows his face, they will arrest him."

She glanced at the Texas cowboy. "You don't know Marc. He has access to other vehicles. He's resourceful. He'll slip through the net. He has nothing to lose at this point. He will be even more dangerous."

"You don't have any idea where your brother-in-law might go?"

She shook her head, then winced in pain. "The man is crazy. Who knows what he'll do now."

"Whatever information he was trying to get out of your sister…he didn't get it, right?"

"No," she said, her eyes filling with tears. "Apparently Rebecca would rather die than tell him."

"I'm trying to understand all of this. Marc Stewart brought you to the cabin to make your sister talk, right? He thought she would tell you. Did she?"

Gillian wiped her tears. "No. Rebecca knew the mo-ment I saw what he'd done to her that I would have told him anything he wanted to know. She didn't tell me *any-thing*. I didn't know about any ledger or about Andy being gone until Marc told me. I'm just praying she regains consciousness soon and tells us where we can find Andy. My nephew is only ten months old…."

"Maybe Marc will turn himself in given that he's wounded and now wanted by the law."

She scoffed at that. "I highly doubt that since what-ever is in this ledger Rebecca took would apparently put

Marc behind bars for years. He'd never go down without a fight."

"A lot of criminals say that—until it comes time to die and then they find they prefer to turn state's evidence," Austin said. "Your sister never even hinted what Marc might be up to?"

"No. I knew they were having trouble. I couldn't understand why she stayed with the man. He was domineering and tight with the money, and treated Rebecca as if she was his property. But I never dreamed something like this would happen. When Rebecca texted me that she had left Marc, I was shocked since there had been no warning."

AUSTIN GLANCED OVER at her as he drove. Gillian looked numb. Her face was still pale, her eyes red from crying. He hated to ask, but he needed to know what they were up against. "Would you mind telling me how all this began?"

She sat up a little straighter, drawing on some inner strength that impressed him. He knew given what she'd been through, she must be exhausted let alone physically injured and emotionally spent.

"I had no idea what was going on. Rebecca and Andy had been at my house just a week before and everything seemed to be fine. Then I got the text. When I saw her car pull up to my house last night, I ran out thinking it was her."

He listened to her explain that instead of it being her sister in the car, it had been Marc. She told him how Marc had thrown her into the trunk and she'd escaped partway down the canyon.

"So there *had* been someone in the trunk," he said. It all made sense now. Even as confused as she'd been after her car accident, she'd recalled someone in the trunk.

"I wasn't thinking clearly when I took off. I just knew I had to get away from Marc and find my sister."

"You did everything you could to save her without any thought to your own life," Austin said. "This is on Marc, not you. But there is one thing I don't understand. Why did your sister choose now to leave him? I mean, had something happened between them?"

Gillian sighed. "I don't know. All I can figure is that Rebecca got her hands on Marc's business ledger, saw what was inside and realized she was married to a criminal—as well as an abuser. Apparently there was a reference to all the money Marc had stashed in the ledger and that's why she went to the Island Park cabin and he followed her there." She shook her head. "I don't know what she was thinking. How could she not know what Marc would do?"

"It sounds as if she was just trying to keep her son safe from him," Austin said. "She was also trying to protect you by not telling you anything." He felt Gillian's gaze on him.

"I'm sorry I dragged you into this."

"We're past that. As I told you before, I'm a deputy sheriff down in Texas. I'm glad I can help."

"I wish you could help, but I have no idea where my sister hid her son, let alone this ledger that Marc is losing his mind over. Marc will only be worse now. He's dangerous and desperate. I'm afraid of what he will do— especially if he finds his son."

Austin hated the truth he heard in her words. He'd known men like Marc Stewart. "Which is another reason I don't want to let you out of my sight. It won't make any difference if he believes your sister told you anything or not. He'll blame you."

"He already does for involving you in this. I'm so sorry. But I can't ask you—"

"I'm in this with you," he said, reaching over to take her hand. He gave it a squeeze and let go.

Gillian met his gaze. Her eyes shimmered with tears. "If you hadn't shown up when you did…" She looked away. He could tell she was fighting tears, worried about her sister and her nephew, and maybe finally realizing how close she had come to dying back there. "I have to find Andy and this notebook, ledger, whatever it is, before Marc does. If he finds it first, he'll skip the country with Andy. I know him. I wouldn't be surprised if he doesn't have a new identity all set up."

MARC AVOIDED LOOKING in the mirror as he drove. His friend had fixed him up. But when he saw his bandaged face in the mirror, it made him furious all over again. And when he was furious, he couldn't think straight.

He'd just assumed that Rebecca would cave at some point and tell him what he wanted to know. Frankly, he'd never thought her a strong woman. Boy, had she proven him wrong, he thought as he silently cursed her to hell. If she had just told him what he wanted to know all this would be over by now. She might even still be alive. Or not. But at least he would have made her death look like an accident.

Word was going to get out about Rebecca's murder. His DNA would be found at the scene. Not to mention he'd shot at a Texas deputy. Gillian would swear he'd kidnapped her… How had things gotten so out of hand? He had a target on his back now. Even with an old pickup and a change of identity, he couldn't risk getting stopped even for a broken taillight—not with this bandage down the side of his face.

His cell phone rang. "What?"

"You don't have to bite off my head."

Marc rolled his eyes, but bit his tongue. He needed his friend's help. "Sorry, Leo. What did you find out?"

"They took your wife to the hospital in Bozeman. I couldn't get any information, though, on her condition."

Rebecca was *alive?*

"As for your sister-in-law? She and some cowboy left together after spending a whole lot of time talking to the cops. I suspect they're headed to Bozeman and the hospital. You want me to keep following them?"

"The man with her? He's a sheriff's deputy from Texas. He'll know if he is being followed, so no. I'll call you if I need you."

He disconnected, not sure what to do next. When his cell rang, he thought it was Leo again. Instead it was his…so-called partner. In truth, Victor Ramsey ran the show and always had. Marc began to sweat instantly as he picked up.

"What the hell is going on, Marc? Why are there cops after you?"

AT THE HOSPITAL in Bozeman, Gillian was told that her sister was stable and resting. She hadn't regained consciousness, but the doctor promised he would call when she did.

Gillian tried not to let the tidal wave of relief drown out the news. Becky was alive and stable. Once she woke up, she could tell them what they needed to know. But in the meantime…

Down the hallway, she saw Austin on his cell phone and overheard the last of what he was saying as she approached. She felt awful as she realized that he'd come to Montana to see his family and Christmas was just days away…. She didn't know what she would have done without him, though, but she couldn't have him missing a family Christmas because of her.

"Hey," he said, smiling when he saw her. "Good news?"

She nodded. "Becky's still unconscious but stable. Listen, Austin, I already owe you my life and my sister's. Aside from almost getting you killed, now I'm keeping you away from your family who you came all the way to Montana to see and it's almost Christmas."

"I came up for the grand opening of our first Texas Boys Barbecue restaurant in Montana."

"Barbecue?"

He nodded at her surprise. "My brothers and I own a few barbecue joints."

"I thought you said you were a deputy sheriff?"

"I am. My brother Laramie runs the company so the rest of us can do whatever we want." He gave a shrug.

"Cardwell?" Why hadn't she realized who he was? "You're related to Dana Savage?"

"She's my cousin. She and her husband own Cardwell Ranch. My brothers came up to visit her, fell in love with Montana and all but one of them has fallen in love with more than the state and moved here."

"You can't miss this grand opening...."

"Believe me, my family can manage without me. Actually, they're used to it. I'm not good at these family events and I'm not leaving you until Marc is behind bars. You're stuck with me." He smiled. He had an amazing smile that lit up his handsome face and made his dark eyes shine.

She hadn't realized how handsome he was. Maybe because she hadn't taken the time to really look at him. "Are you trying to tell me that you're the black sheep of the family?" she asked as they took the elevator down to the hospital parking area.

He laughed at that. "And then some. I missed my brother Tag's wedding last summer. I was on a case. I'm often on a case. I'm only here now because they all ganged up on me and made me feel guilty."

"When is the grand opening?"

"The first of January. See? Nothing to worry about."

"You're that confident Marc will be caught by then?" she asked.

He turned that smile on her. "With my luck, he will and I won't have any excuse not to attend not only the grand opening but also Christmas at my cousin's house with the whole family."

"You aren't serious."

"On the contrary. I usually volunteer to work the holidays so deputies with families can spend them at home. I'm the worst Scrooge ever when it comes to Christmas. So trust me when I say my family won't be surprised I'm not there, nor will they mind all that much."

"I think you're exaggerating," she said as they reached his SUV.

He shook his head. "Nope. It's the truth. What do you suggest we do now?"

She turned to look at him. "I can't ask you—"

"You aren't asking. I already told you. I'm not leaving you alone until Marc is behind bars."

Tears filled her eyes. She bit down on her lower lip for a moment. "Thank you. I need to go to my house."

"Where is that?"

"I have a studio at Big Sky."

"A studio?"

"I'm a jeweler."

"The watch." He frowned and she could see he was wondering who'd made it for her.

"My father was the one who taught me the craft. I

lost him five years ago. Before that, my mother. I can't lose my sister."

He put an arm around her and pulled her close. "You won't. The doctor said she is stable, right? She's a strong woman and she has every reason to pull through."

Gillian nodded against his strong chest. He smelled of the outdoors, a wonderful masculine scent that reminded her how long it had been since a man had held her. She reminded herself why Austin Cardwell was here with her and stepped away from his arms.

"I need to figure out what my sister was thinking," she said as Austin opened the door to the SUV. "It was one thing to hide the ledger, but another to hide my nephew."

As he slid behind the wheel, he asked, "Those few moments you had with your sister before Marc returned, did she say anything that might have been a clue where either might be?"

"I'm not even sure she was in her right mind at the end. Marc told me she was taking some kind of pills for stress before all this happened."

Austin shook his head as he started the engine. "She got her son away from Marc and she hid a book that can possibly get her husband put away for a long time. On top of that, she wounded Marc in a way that makes him easy to spot. That doesn't sound like a woman who wasn't thinking straight."

Gillian's eyes filled with tears. "But why didn't she tell me where to find Andy and the ledger?"

"Maybe she mailed you something. Or said something that didn't make sense at the time, but will later. You've been through so much, not to mention Marc taking you out of the hospital too soon after a head injury. You say you live at Big Sky?"

"Before you get to Meadow Village. I have an apartment over my studio and shop." She rubbed her temples with her fingers.

"Headache?"

Gillian nodded. "Maybe Becky *did* send me something in the mail. If that's the case…" She turned to look at him. "Then we need to get to my house before Marc does."

THEY WERE ONLY a few miles out of Big Sky when Gillian fell into an exhausted sleep. Austin's heart went out to her. He couldn't imagine what the past forty-eight hours had been like for her. He worried about her even though she was holding up better than he would have expected. The woman was strong. Or maybe it hadn't really hit her yet.

What drove him was the thought of Marc Stewart not just getting away with kidnapping and attempted murder, but possibly finding his son and taking him out of the country. If that happened, Austin doubted either Rebecca or her sister would ever see the child again.

The man had to be stopped, and Austin was determined to do what he could to make that happen.

When Gillian woke near the outskirts of Big Sky, she looked better, definitely more determined. There was so much more he needed to know about the situation he'd found himself in and he was anxious to ask. But first they had to reach her studio. There was the chance that Marc Stewart had been there—was even still there.

Chapter Thirteen

Marc held the phone away from his ear for a moment as he considered how much to tell Victor. The first time Marc had met Victor Ramsey, he'd been amused by the man's clean-cut appearance that belied the true man underneath. That was five years ago. Victor still had one of those trustworthy faces, bright blue eyes and a winning smile. But if you looked deeper into those blue eyes, as Marc had done too many times, you would see a cold-blooded psychopath.

"What's going on, Marc?" Victor asked now as if he'd just called to catch up.

The two had met through a mutual friend, something Marc later suspected had been a setup from the start.

Want to make more money than you've ever dreamed possible? his friend had said one night after they'd consumed too much alcohol.

His answer had been, *Hell yes.* The auto body shop he'd taken over from his father was a lot of work and for average income, not to mention he hated it.

His friend, now deceased under suspicious circumstances, had made the introduction. At first Marc had been in awe of Victor, a self-made man with a lot of charm and ambition. It wasn't until he was in too deep that he'd begun to regret all of it.

"Just having a little domestic trouble," Marc answered now.

"Attempted murder is a little more than domestic trouble. I want to see you. Where are you?"

He'd been expecting this, but the last person he wanted to see him like this was Victor. "Right now isn't a great time."

"I'm staying at my place in Canyon Creek. I'll give you two hours. Don't be late. You know how I hate anyone who wastes my time." Victor hung up.

Marc swore. After Victor saw his face—and found out everything else—Marc knew he would be lucky to walk out of that meeting alive.

With a curse, he realized he had really only one choice. Get out of the country—or at least try. But it would mean leaving without his son—or settling the score with his wife, his sister-in-law and the Texas deputy who'd stuck his nose in where it didn't belong.

He would prefer to find the ledger and his son, take care of all of them and then get out of the country. Rebecca had discovered some of his money, but he had more hidden.

Unfortunately the clock was ticking and if he hoped to live long enough to do what had to be done, he would have to meet with Victor and try to talk his way out of this mess.

AUSTIN PARKED BEHIND a three-story building with a sign that read Gillian Cooper Designs. As she led the way up the back steps, Austin kept an eye out for Marc Stewart. There was no sign of his black Suburban, but Austin figured he would have gotten rid of it by now.

There were no other buildings around Gillian's. The studio and apartment sat against the mountainside with only one parking spot in back. The building was unique in design. When he asked her about it, he wasn't surprised to find out that she'd designed it herself.

As she led him into the living area, he saw that the inside was as uniquely designed as the outside with shiny bamboo floors, vaulted wood ceilings, arches and tall windows. He could see that she had more than just a talent for jewelry. The decor was a mixture of old and new, each room bright with color and texture.

Remembering how Marc had torn up the Island Park cabin, he was relieved to see that the man hadn't been in Gillian's apartment. From what he could gather, nothing had been disturbed. Maybe Marc had been wounded badly enough that he'd been forced to get medical attention before anything else. Once an emergency room doctor saw the bullet wound, the law would be called and Marc would be arrested. At least Austin could hope.

He stood in the living area, taking in the place. He found himself becoming more intrigued by Gillian Cooper as he watched her scoop up the mail that had been dropped through the old-fashioned slot in the antique front door.

"I love your house," he said, hoping he got a chance to see the jewelry she made.

"Thanks," she said as she sorted through the mail. He could tell by her disappointed expression that there was nothing from her sister. She looked up at him. "Nothing." Her voice broke as she shook her head.

"Why don't you get a hot shower and a change of clothes," he suggested.

She nodded. "There is a shower in the guest room if you…"

"Thank you." They stood like that for a moment, strangers who knew too much about each other, bound together by happenstance.

He moved first, picking up his duffel bag, which he'd brought up from the car. She pointed toward an open door as if no longer capable of speech. He'd seen it often in people who were thrown into extraordinary circumstances. They often found an inner strength that made it possible for them to do extraordinary things. But at some point that strength ebbed away, leaving them an empty shell.

The shower was hot, the water pressure strong. Austin stood under it, spent. He'd had little sleep last night and then today… He was just thankful he'd burst into the cabin when he had. He didn't want to think what would have happened otherwise. Nor did he want to think about what he'd gotten himself into and where it would end.

CLEAN AND WARM and dressed in clean jeans and a long-sleeved T-shirt, Austin went back out into the living room. Where was Marc now? Austin could only imagine. Hopefully he'd been arrested, but if that were the case, Austin would have received a call by now. The officer who'd responded to his call had promised to let him know when Marc Stewart was in custody.

Which meant Marc Stewart was still out there.

A few minutes later, Gillian emerged from the other side of the house. Her face was flushed from her shower. She wore a white fluffy sweater and leggings. Her long dark hair was still damp and framed the face of a model.

For a moment, she looked nervous, as if realizing she was now alone with a complete stranger.

"If you don't mind talking about it, could you tell me more about this ledger Marc is looking for?" he said, finding ground he knew would ease the sudden tension between them.

"I only know what Marc told me," she said as she walked to the refrigerator, opened it and held up a bottle of wine. He nodded and she poured two glasses, which they took into the living room.

Gillian curled up at one end of the couch, tucking her feet under her. Austin took a chair some distance away. He watched her take a sip of her wine and she seemed to relax a little.

"I gathered Marc wrote down some sort of illegal business dealings in a black ledger that he never let out of his sight," she said after a moment. "Marc is dyslexic so he has trouble remembering numbers, apparently. He wrote everything down. According to him, my sister drugged him and took the book."

"What do you know about your brother-in-law's business?"

"Nothing really. He owns an auto body shop, repairs cars."

"That doesn't sound like something that would force him to go to the extremes he has to recover some ledger he kept figures in."

"I'm not sure what's in it other than where he hid large amounts of money, but I gathered, from Marc's terror at the ledger landing in the wrong hands, that there is enough in it to send him to prison."

"I don't understand why she didn't take it to the police or the FBI. Marc would be in jail now and none of this would have happened."

Gillian shook her head. "Apparently she thought she could force him into giving her a divorce and custody of Andrew Marc in exchange for the ledger. She also needed money. I guess she didn't realize just how dangerous that would be."

"Or she didn't get a chance to before Marc realized the ledger was missing. He figured out she was headed for the Island Park cabin fairly quickly."

She nodded. "He'd stashed money there." She grew quiet for a moment. "Apparently she hid the ledger. I know it's not at their house. He said he tore the place apart looking for it."

"You and your sister were close. Any ideas where she could have hidden it?"

"None. Becky and I…" She hesitated, turning to glance out the side window. "We weren't that close recently. Marc thought I was a bad influence on her. I didn't want to make things worse for her but I couldn't stand being around him. He kept her on a short leash. The last time we were together before this, I begged her to leave Marc. She kept thinking he was going to change."

Austin heard the worry in her voice. "A lot of women have trouble leaving."

"I always thought my sister was smarter than that," she said as she got up to refill their glasses.

"Intelligence doesn't seem to have much to do with it." He doubted this helped at the moment. Marc Stewart was out there somewhere, wounded and still obsessed with finding not only the ledger, but also his son. Which meant Gillian wasn't safe until Marc was behind bars and maybe not even then, depending on just what Marc Stewart was involved in.

She met his gaze as she filled his glass. "You saw what Marc's like. Just out of spite, he might do something to Andy if he finds him." Her voice cracked, and for a moment, she looked as if she might break down.

Austin rose to take her in his arms. She felt small but

strong. It was he who felt vulnerable. He'd never met anyone like her, and that scared him. Not to mention the fact that Gillian felt too good in his arms.

He let go of her and she stepped away to wipe her tears.

"We'll find your nephew," he said to her back. He had no idea how, but he agreed with her. Marc was a loose cannon now. Anyone in his path was in danger. "Your sister was living in Helena? Where would she stash her son that she thought he would be safe? Marc said the boy was with his grandmother."

Gillian shook her head. "No grandparents are still alive."

"Maybe a babysitter? A friend she trusted?"

Again Gillian shook her head. "Marc didn't allow her to leave Andy with anyone, not that she had need of a babysitter because he would check on her during the day to make sure she hadn't gone anywhere."

Austin hated the picture she was painting of her sister's life. "Then how did your sister manage to not only get possession of Marc's ledger, but hide their son?"

Gillian shook her head again. "I suspect she'd been planning it for weeks, maybe even months. Rebecca did tell me when I was trying to get her to leave him that time in Helena that Marc had threatened to kill her and Andy if she did."

He guessed that Rebecca had believed her husband. But then she'd taken the ledger and thought she had leverage. "You said your sister visited a while back. Is there a chance she left you a note that you might have missed?"

Gillian shook her head and stepped to one of the windows to look out. Past her, he caught glimpses of the Gallatin River and the dense snowcapped pines. It was snowing again, huge flakes drifting down past the window. How could his brothers live in a place where it snowed like this?

"Apparently my sister found quite a bit of money that Marc kept hidden in his locked gun cabinet." She turned toward him. "It is missing, as well."

He thought of the ransacked Island Park cabin. "Your sister had gone to the cabin to get more money he had stashed there?"

She nodded. "So foolish. I guess she wanted to keep him from skipping the country and taking his money, and she thought that would work. She apparently didn't think she could keep him in jail long enough to do whatever she had planned."

He watched her look around the room as if remembering her sister's last visit. She frowned. "If Becky was well into her plan when she came to see me, why didn't she say something? Why didn't she tell me so I would know what to do now?" She sounded close to tears again.

"While she was here, where did she stay?"

"In the spare bedroom. You don't think she might have hidden the ledger in there?"

He followed her, thinking there was a remote chance at best. Still, they had to look. Like the rest of the place, it was nicely furnished in an array of colors. The wall behind the bed was exposed brick. Several pieces of artwork hung from it.

Gillian searched the room from the drawers in the bedside tables to under the mattress and even under the bed. Austin went into the bathroom and looked in the only cabinet there. No note or a ledger of any kind.

As Gillian finished, she sat down on the end of the bed. She looked pale and exhausted, like a woman who should be in the hospital.

"Are you sure you shouldn't have seen a doctor while we were at the hospital? I don't mind taking you back."

"I'm fine," she said with a sigh. "Just disappointed. I knew it was doubtful that Becky left anything. She would have been afraid I would find it and try to stop her. Rebecca never wanted to be a bother to anyone, especially me, her older sister. She hid a lot of things from me, like just how bad it was living with Marc."

"Why don't you get some rest? We can talk more in the morning and figure out what to do next."

She nodded. "I can't even think straight right now."

He reached out and took her hand to pull her up from the bed. "You still have that headache?"

She smiled at him. "It's nothing to be alarmed about. I'm fine. Really." Suddenly she froze. "Becky *did* leave something." Her voice rose with excitement. "I didn't think anything about it at the time. Since Andy had been playing with an old key ring of hers that had a dozen keys on it. She left a key on the night table beside the bed. I thought it must have come off Andy's key ring so I just tossed it in the drawer for when he came back."

She opened the drawer beside the bed and took out the key.

Austin had hoped for a safety deposit key. Instead, it appeared to be an ordinary house key. He realized that Gillian's first instinct on finding it was probably right.

"You didn't find anything else?"

She shook her head, her excitement fading. "It's probably nothing, huh?"

"Probably," he said, taking the key. "But we'll hang on to it just in case." He pocketed it as Gillian started to leave the room.

"You can have this room," she said over her shoulder.

She stopped in the doorway and turned to look back at him. "That is, if you're staying."

"As I told you, I'm not going anywhere until Marc is behind bars. I'm a man of my word, Gillian."

She met his gaze. "Somehow I knew that."

"No matter how long it takes, I'm not leaving you." Austin knew even as he made the promise that there would be hell to pay with his family. But they were used to him letting them down. She started to turn away.

"One more thing," he said. "Did your sister have a key to this house?"

"No." Realization dawned on her expression. She shivered.

"Then there is nothing to worry about," he said. "Try to get some sleep."

"You, too."

He knew that wouldn't be easy. An electricity seemed to spark in the air between them. They'd been through so much together already. He didn't dare imagine what tomorrow would bring.

She hesitated in the doorway. "If you need anything…"

"Don't worry about me." As he removed his jacket, her gaze went to the weapon in his shoulder holster. He saw her swallow before she turned away. "Sweet dreams," he said to her retreating back.

Chapter Fourteen

It had begun to snow. Large lacy flakes fell in a flurry of white as Marc pulled up to Victor's so-called cabin in the mountains overlooking Helena, Montana. The "cabin" was at least five thousand square feet of luxury including an indoor pool, a media center and a game room. At his knock, one of Victor's minions answered the door, a big man who went by only Jumbo.

"Mr. Ramsey is in the garden room." Oh, yeah, and the house had a garden room, too.

There was no garden in the glassed-in room, but there was an amazing view of the valley below and there was a bar. Victor was standing at the bar pouring himself a drink. Marc got the feeling he'd seen him drive up and had been waiting. Today he wore a velour pullover in the same blue as his eyes.

"What would you like to drink?" he asked as he motioned to one of the chairs at the bar. Victor seemed to take in his bandaged face and neck, but said nothing.

Marc took one of the chairs. "Whatever you're having."

"Wise man," Victor said with a disarming smile. "I only drink the best. Isn't that the reason you and I became friends to begin with?"

Friends? What a joke. Marc didn't need him to spell things out. "I like the best things in life like anyone else."

"But you aren't like anyone else," Victor said as he pushed what looked like three fingers of bourbon in a crystal glass over to him.

"No, I'm unique because I know you." He knew it was what the man wanted to hear, and right now he was fine with saying anything that could get him out of here. He took a gulp of the drink. It burned all the way down. As he set the glass down, he said, "Okay, I screwed up, but I'm trying to fix it."

Victor lifted a brow. "You think? And how is it you hope to do that?"

He wasn't surprised that his mess was no secret to the man. Victor had someone inside law enforcement. There was little he didn't know about.

"I didn't mean to almost kill her."

"The her you're referring to being your *wife?*"

"Who else?"

"Who else indeed. With you I never know." Victor took a sip of his drink, studying him over the rim of the glass. "Attempted murder, kidnapping, assault?" Victor leaned on the bar like one friend confiding in another. "Tell me, Marc. What's going on with you?"

He knew this tone of voice. He'd seen it used on other men who'd messed up in their little…organization. He also knew what had happened to those men. Victor was most dangerous when he was being congenial.

"The bitch drugged me and took my ledger—you know, where I kept track of the business."

Victor leaned back, his expression making it clear that his concern had shifted to himself rather than Marc's future. "By the business, you mean your automotive business."

Marc didn't answer.

"You wrote down *our* business transactions?"

"It was a lot of names and numbers, and I do better if I can write it down."

"You mean like names of our associates and their phone numbers." His voice had dropped even further.

"Yeah, that and a few transactions just so I could remember whom I'd dealt with. You have a lot of associates."

Victor looked as if he might have a coronary. "This... ledger? I'm assuming you got it back. Tell me you got it back."

"Why do you think I tried to kill her? She hid it *and* my kid. I was trying to get the information out of her...."

"That's why you involved her sister." Victor closed his eyes for a moment. He was breathing hard. Marc had never seen him lose his cool. Victor was the kind of man who didn't do his own dirty work. He prided himself on never losing control, but he seemed close right now.

"So you don't have the information and you don't know where it is," Victor said.

That about sized it up. "But I'm going to find it."

"She could have mailed it to the FBI."

Marc hadn't thought of that. Probably because he was still caught up in his old belief that Rebecca wasn't all that smart. "I don't think she'd do that."

Victor looked at him, aghast. "You don't *think* so?"

"She's just trying to use the ledger to get a divorce and custody of my kid."

"Let me guess." Victor didn't look at him. Instead, he turned his glass in his hands as if admiring the cut crystal. "You refused to give her what she wanted."

"She isn't taking my kid." The blow took him by surprise. The heavy crystal glass smashed into the side of his face, knocking him off his stool. The crystal shattered, prisms flying across the Italian rock flooring of the garden room an instant before Marc joined them.

Jumbo appeared, as if he had been waiting in the wings, expecting trouble. "You all right, Mr. Ramsey?"

Marc swore. Victor wasn't the one on the floor surrounded by glass. As he rose, he saw Victor picking glass out of his hand. Jumbo rushed around the bar to get a rag.

"No harm done. Isn't that right, Marc?" Victor said.

Blood was running down into his eye. He reached up and pulled a shard of glass from his temple.

"Get Marc a bandage to go with his other bandages, will you, Jumbo?" their boss said. "Sorry about that," he said after Jumbo had left. "I seldom lose my temper."

Marc said nothing. His head hurt like hell and this was the second time in twenty-four hours that he'd been cut. The blow had opened his other cut, and it, too, was now bleeding. First his wife had tried to kill him, now this.

Jumbo returned with a first aid kit. "Let him see to it," Victor ordered when Marc tried to take the kit from the man. It was all he could do to sit still and let an oaf like Jumbo work on him. "Here, be sure there isn't any glass in the cut first." Victor handed the man a bottle of Scotch. "Pour some of the good stuff on it."

Marc gritted his teeth as Jumbo shoved his head to the side and poured the alcohol into the wound. The Scotch ran into Rebecca's handiwork as well, sending fiery pain roaring through him. He swore, the pain so intense he thought he might black out. Jumbo patted the spot on his temple dry with surprising tenderness before carefully applying something to stop the bleeding.

"There, all better," Victor said. "Thank Jumbo. He did a great job."

"Thanks, Jumbo," Marc mumbled.

After Jumbo had cleaned up the mess and left, his boss refilled Marc's glass and got himself a new one. "Now," he said, "I don't need to tell you what needs to be done, do I?"

"No. I'm going to get the ledger." He knew better than to mention his son. Victor didn't give a crap about Andy.

The man frowned. "The sister, is she going to be a problem?"

"Naw." He tried to keep his gaze locked with Victor's, but he broke away first even though he knew it was a mistake.

"The sister isn't the only problem, is she? Who is this Texas deputy who got involved?"

Marc swore under his breath. It amazed him how Victor got his information and so quickly. He must have "associates" everywhere. The thought did nothing to make him feel better.

"I'll take care of them."

Victor shook his head. "You just get this…ledger you lost back. And what are you going to do with it?"

"Destroy it."

Victor looked pained. "Wrong, you're going to bring it to me. I'll take care of it. There are no copies, right?"

"No, I'm not a fool." From Victor's expression, it was clear he thought differently. Marc should have been relieved. What Victor was saying was that they were finished. No more money. It was over. Their relationship was terminated.

Marc searched his emotions for the relief he should have been feeling. Instead, all he could think was that he would kill them. First Rebecca. Then her sister and the cowboy. "I'll fix everything."

Victor didn't look convinced. "Just find the ledger. That's all I ask."

But Marc knew nothing in his life had ever been that simple. He downed his drink, stood up and left.

GILLIAN WENT TO her bedroom, but she doubted she would be able to sleep. Her mind was racing. She kept going over the few conversations she'd had with her sister in the months, weeks and days before all this.

What had Rebecca been thinking? Why hadn't she taken the incriminating evidence to the police? Had she really thought Marc would just agree to a divorce?

No, she thought. That's why Rebecca had hidden not only the ledger, but also her son.

As she pulled on a nightgown and climbed into bed, she was reminded that she wasn't alone in the house. That should have given her more comfort than it did. She was very...aware of Austin Cardwell. It surprised her that she could feel anything, as exhausted and distraught as she was. Mostly, she felt...off balance.

She closed her eyes, praying for the oblivion of sleep.

"I might need your help."

Gillian's eyes came open as she recalled something her sister had said. The conversation came back to her slowly.

"You know I will do anything for you."

"I don't like involving you, but if things go wrong..."

"Becky, what's going on?"

"I keep thinking about when we were kids."

"You're scaring me."

"I'm sorry. I was just being sentimental."

"Is everything okay, Becky?"

"Yes," her sister said, laughing. *"I was just remembering how much fun it was growing up. I love you, Gillian. Always remember that."*

Oh, Becky, she thought now as tears filled her eyes. Things had gone very wrong. Unfortunately, Gillian had no idea what to do about it and now she had a Texas cowboy in her spare bedroom.

She wasn't going to get a wink of sleep tonight.

MARC SCRATCHED THE back of his neck and glanced in the rearview mirror. He caught sight of a large gray SUV two cars behind him. Without slowing, he drove from Victor's toward downtown Helena. At the very last minute, he swung off the interstate and glanced back in time to see the gray SUV cross two lanes to make the exit.

He sped up, wanting to lose the tail. That damned Victor. He'd put a man on him. Marc shouldn't have been surprised. Had he been Victor, he wouldn't have trusted him either. Victor had to know that with the ledger and his testimony, his "friend" Marc could walk away from this mess a free man while Victor rotted in prison.

Not that Victor would let him live long enough for that to happen.

Swearing, he slowed down and pulled into a gas station. He saw the gray SUV go past to stop a few doors down in front of a fast-food restaurant. Getting out, he filled his tank and considered what to do next.

His throat felt dry. He would kill for a beer. The problem was stopping at just one beer. It would be too easy to get falling-down drunk. Still, he headed for one of the bars he frequented. Behind him, the gray SUV followed.

Victor's going to have me killed.

Not until I find the ledger.

The thought turned Marc's blood to ice.

But it was quickly followed by another thought.

In the meantime, Victor couldn't chance that the ledger would turn up and fall into the wrong hands. *Checkmate,* he thought with relief until he had another thought.

Unless Victor decided he could do a better job of getting the whereabouts of the book from Rebecca.

That thought echoed in his head, making his heart thump harder against his chest. Marc felt the truth of those words racing through his bloodstream. What if Victor decided to take things into his own hands?

He thought of Rebecca lying in her hospital bed. If Victor paid her one of his famous visits…

Marc reminded himself that Victor never got his own hands dirty even if he could find a way to get near Rebecca in the hospital.

What if Rebecca really had mailed the ledger to the FBI? His pulse jumped, heart hammering like a sledge in his chest. He wouldn't let himself go there. No, she'd hidden the book thinking she was smarter than he was, thinking she could force him into the divorce and take Andy from him. Stupid woman.

He tried to concentrate on what to do now. Because if she hadn't sent the book to the FBI, he had to assume she didn't know what she had in her possession. That was the good news, right?

The bad news was that no matter the outcome, he and Victor were finished. Even if he found the book and turned it over, Victor would never trust him again. Not that he could blame him. The information in that book could bring them all down. Victor would have him killed.

If he didn't find the ledger and the cops did, he was going to prison for a good part of the rest of his life. Of course that life wouldn't be long since Victor and his buddies would be in prison with him.

He still couldn't believe the mess he was in. He realized there was only one way out of this. He had to get to Rebecca before Victor did. Once she understood the consequences if she didn't turn over the ledger…he'd give her the divorce and custody. She would hand over his ledger and then when she thought she was safe, he would kidnap his kid and skip the country.

Why hadn't he thought of that in the first place? Because the woman had made him so furious. Also, he'd thought she would tell him where the ledger was with only minor persuasion.

He parked beside the bar in a dark spot away from the streetlamp and put in a call to the hospital. Rebecca was still unconscious. Swearing, he hung up.

The clock was ticking.

Inside the bar, Marc Stewart took a stool away from everyone else and ordered a beer. The bartender gave him a raised eyebrow at his bandaged face and the black eye that was almost swollen shut, but was smart enough not to comment.

The first beer went down easy. The second took a little longer. He was doing a lot of thinking. Mostly about Rebecca and how he'd underestimated her. He kept mentally kicking himself. He had to get over her betrayal and think about what to do.

"Another beer?" the bartender asked as he cleared away his second empty bottle.

Marc focused on an old moose head hanging on the wall behind the bartender that could have used a good dusting. It reminded him of something. "No, I'm good," he told the bartender. Something about the moose head still nagged at him, but his head hurt too badly to make sense of it.

He slid off the bar stool, picked up most of his change from the bar and pocketed it. But as he looked toward the door, he told himself he had to ditch the tail that he knew would be parked outside waiting.

Marc smiled to himself even though it hurt his face to do so and put in the call. It was time to take care of business.

Chapter Fifteen

Gillian thought she would never be able to sleep again. At the very least she'd expected to have horrible nightmares.

She must have fallen into a deathlike sleep. She couldn't remember anything. Now, though, it all came back in a rush, including the Texas cowboy in her spare bedroom.

What did she really know about Austin Cardwell? Nothing. Nothing except he'd saved her life twice and made her feel… She wasn't even sure how to describe it other than she felt too aware of the man.

She caught the smell of bacon cooking. *Austin?* Grabbing her robe, she opened her door to find him standing in her kitchen with a pancake flipper in his hand. He was wearing one of her aprons, which actually made her smile.

"You didn't find bacon in my refrigerator," she said.

He turned to smile back at her. "Nope. Apparently you exist on wine."

"I haven't gotten to the store in a while."

"I noticed." He flipped over what she saw were pancakes sizzling on her griddle. "Hungry?"

She started to say she wasn't. Just as she'd thought she'd never be able to sleep again, she thought the same of eating. But her stomach growled loudly at the smell of bacon and pancakes.

Austin chuckle. "I'll take that as a yes." He motioned for her to have a seat at the breakfast bar.

"I should change," she said, pulling the collar of her robe tighter.

"No need. Eat them while they're hot." He slid a tall stack of three-inch pancakes onto her plate along with two slices of bacon. "This is my mother's recipe for corn cakes. It's the Texan in me. Wait until you taste the eggs. I hope you like hot peppers."

She felt her eyes widen in surprise. "You made eggs, as well? I really can't—"

"Insult me by not trying some?"

She couldn't help but smile at him in all his eagerness. "Are you trying to fatten me up?"

"You could use a little Texas cooking—not that you aren't beautiful just as you are."

"Good catch," she said, knowing it wasn't true. She hadn't been taking good care of herself because she'd been so worried about her sister. "Thank you."

"My pleasure." He joined her, loading his plate with pancakes, bacon and eggs before putting a spoonful of the eggs onto her plate. "Just try them. Some people aren't tough enough to handle my cooking."

It sounded like a dare—just as he'd meant it to. She studied him for a moment. What would she have done without him? Died night before last in the snowstorm beside the road and no doubt yesterday in Island Park.

Austin handed her the peach jam he'd bought. "Try some of this on your pancakes. Much better than maple syrup."

"Why not?" she said, doing as he said.

"Now take a bite of the pancake and one of the egg. Sweet and hot."

She did and felt her eyes widen in alarm for a moment at the heat. But he was right. The sweet cooled it right down. "Delicious."

"Now add a bite of bacon for saltiness and you've got an Austin Cardwell Texas breakfast." He laughed as he took a bite, chewed and, closing his eyes, moaned in obvious contentment.

Gillian was caught up in his enjoyment of breakfast and her own, as well. She couldn't remember the last time she'd eaten like this and was shocked when she realized that she'd cleaned her plate.

"Well?" he said, studying her openly. "Feeling better?"

She was. Earlier when she'd awakened, she'd felt lightheaded and sick to her stomach. Now she was ready to do whatever had to be done to save her nephew, and she was pretty sure that had been Austin's plan.

"DON'T YOU DARE tell me you lost him," Victor said when he saw who was calling that morning.

"Sorry, boss. He let me think he knew he was being tailed and had accepted it."

He swore, but quickly calmed back down. He hadn't gotten where he was by losing control. True, Marc had already pushed him to the point of losing his temper. Marc Stewart had been a mistake. When he'd first met him, Marc had impressed him. He'd seemed like a man who had all his ducks in a row. That, added to the man's hunger for the finer things in life, and his charm and willingness to bend the rules, had made him a perfect associate.

Even when he'd realized the man had his flaws, he'd told himself that most men did. Unfortunately, the flaw Victor hadn't seen in Marc Stewart was about to bring them all down.

"Marc won't get far from home," Victor said. "John, I need you to watch his auto shop. Get Ray to keep an eye on the Friendly Bar over on the south side of town. It's Marc's go-to bar when things aren't going well. If either of you spot him again, stay on him. Trade off. Don't lose him again."

He hung up, hating that he hadn't put Jumbo on him. Jumbo wouldn't have lost him. Victor had realized last night after talking to Marc that he couldn't trust anyone with this, especially Marc. He'd already bungled things.

Changing into a clean sport shirt and a pair of jeans, Victor pulled on his lucky buffalo-skin boots and checked himself in the mirror. His unthreatening good looks had always served him well. He hoped they didn't let him down when he went to visit Rebecca Stewart at the hospital in Bozeman.

IT WAS GOOD to see some color in Gillian's face as they finished cleaning up the breakfast dishes together and she excused herself. Last night Austin had been worried he was going to have to take her back to the hospital. He was surprised she'd even been on her feet after the car wreck, the concussion and yesterday's events, not to mention Marc knocking her around before that. Her strength and endurance surprised him and filled him with admiration. If he had almost lost one of his brothers…

The thought was a punch to the gut and a wake-up call. He realized that he'd taken his four brothers for granted, assuming they would always be there.

He pulled out his cell phone and dialed his cousin Dana. He didn't want to have a long discussion with any one of his brothers. He knew it was cowardice on his part, but at the same time, he wanted to let them know he was all right and that he would try to make Christmas and the grand opening.

Actually, he didn't want to have to explain himself to anyone, even his cousin Dana. He'd hoped he would get her answering machine and he groaned inwardly when she answered on the third ring.

"Hey, Dana. It's Austin, your cousin?"

"The elusive Austin Cardwell? Hud said he met you, but I haven't had that opportunity yet."

"Sorry, but I'm afraid it could be a while yet."

She chuckled. "Hud said not to expect you for dinner until I saw the whites of your eyes."

"Your husband is one smart man."

"Yes, he is. I suppose you're calling me with a message for your brothers."

"Hud's wife is pretty sharp, as well."

She laughed. "What would you like me to tell them?"

Austin thought about that for a moment. "I'll try to make Christmas, but if I don't…"

"They're determined you will be at the grand opening. They're going to put it off until you're here. Don't see any way out for you."

"I guess it's too much to hope they'll go ahead without me if I don't show."

"Yep. Should I tell them you'll be getting back to them?"

"Tell them…I'll see them as soon as I can. You, too. If I can make Christmas, I will be there with bells on."

"Your cabin will be ready."

"EVERYTHING ALL RIGHT?" Gillian asked as she saw him pocket his cell phone.

"Fine. I talked to my cousin. She'll let my brothers know that I've been…detained."

She hated that he already had problems with his brothers and now she was making it worse. He followed her into the living room, the two of them sitting as they had the night before. "Are your parents still alive?"

He nodded. "Divorced. I was born in Montana, but my mother took all five of us boys to Texas when we were very young. My father stayed in Montana. Now my mother has remarried, and she and her new husband just bought a place near here where three of my brothers are living." He shrugged.

"You're lucky to have such a large family. After we lost our parents, it was just Becky and me. With her…" She fought the stark emotion that had her praying one moment and wanting to just sit down and bawl the next.

"I'm sure you already called the hospital. How is she doing?"

"There's been no change, but the doctor did say she is stable and he is hopeful. Have you ever lost anyone close to you?"

"A friend and fellow deputy." Austin hadn't gone a day in years without thinking about Mitch. "He was like a brother." He'd been even closer to Mitch than he was to his brothers. "He was killed in the line of duty. I wasn't there that day." And he'd never forgiven himself for it. He'd been away on barbecue company business.

"I'm sure it gets better," she said hopefully.

He nodded. "It does and it doesn't. You can never fill that hole in your life. Or your heart. But you put one foot in front of the other and you go on. Your sister, though, is going to come back."

"I hope you're right." She cleared her throat. "Right now I can't imagine how to go on. I'd hoped Becky had left me a letter, some kind of message…." Her voice broke.

"Tell me what you remember she said in what time you did have with her yesterday. It might help."

Shaking her head, she got up and walked to the opening into the living room. The December day glistened with fresh snow and sunshine. The bright sunlight poured through the leaded glass windows. Prisms of color sparkled in almost blinding light. She'd always loved this room because of the morning sunlight, but not even the sun's rays could warm her right now.

"Becky talked about our childhood."

"Where did you grow up?"

"In Helena. But we spent our summers at our grandfather's cabin. My sister mentioned the time the wind blew down an old pine tree in a thunderstorm. Becky and I loved thunderstorms and used to huddle together on Grandpa's porch and watch the lightning and the waves crashing on the shore." A lump formed in her throat. She couldn't lose her sister.

"Where is your grandfather's cabin?"

"Outside of Townsend on Canyon Ferry Lake."

"You think your nephew is at your grandfather's cabin?"

She shook her head. "The cabin's been boarded up for years. That's why what she said doesn't make any sense."

"Maybe she left you a message there," Austin suggested. "The only place she mentioned was the cabin, right?"

Gillian nodded.

"If your sister was in her right mind enough to hide her son and try to get Marc Stewart out of his life, then anything she said might have value. Can we get to the cabin this time of year?"

"The road should be open. They get a lot less snow up there than we do down here."

"What is the chance Marc knows about the cabin and will go there?" Austin asked.

She felt a start. "If he remembers it... I think Becky took him there once when they were dating. Since it was nothing like his family's place in Island Park, I don't think he was impressed."

"I suspect there is a reason your sister reminded you of the downed tree and your grandfather's cabin. How soon can you be ready to leave?"

Chapter Sixteen

Marc watched his side mirror as he drove toward Townsend, Montana. His mind seemed sharper this morning. His face still hurt like hell, though. He'd changed the bandage himself, shocked at the damage his wife had done and all the more determined to kill her.

Last night, he'd managed to lose his tail and find a cheap motel at the edge of town, where he'd fallen asleep the instant his head hit the pillow.

It was this morning after a shower that he'd thought of that old moose head he'd seen at the bar and remembered his wife's family's cabin. Rebecca had taken him to see it when they were dating. As far as he knew, though, Rebecca and her sister still owned the place.

She'd been all weepy and sentimental because the cabin had belonged to her grandfather who'd died. Apparently she and her sister had spent summers there with the old man. He didn't get the weepy, emotional significance of the small old place in the pines. That was probably why he'd forgotten about it. That and the fact that they'd never returned to the place.

But he was good at getting back to a place he'd only been to once. He paid attention even when someone else was driving. Given how his wife felt about the old cabin, wasn't it possible she might return there when she had something to stash?

He drove toward the lake. The sleep had helped. He felt more confident that he could pull himself out of this mess. Ahead, he saw a sign that looked familiar and began to slow. If Rebecca had hidden the ledger at the cabin—which he was betting was a real possibility—then he would know soon enough.

Marc hoped his instincts were right as he turned off the main highway and headed down the dirt road back into the mountains along the lake. It had snowed so there was a fine dusting on the road, but nothing to worry about. This area never got as much snow as those closer to the mountains.

The road was the least of his worries anyway. He thought of Gillian and the cowboy deputy. Would Gillian think of the cabin?

Swearing under his breath, he realized that if he had, then she would, too. Maybe she was already there. Maybe she already had her hands on the ledger. The thought sent his pulse into overdrive.

But as he turned onto the narrow road that led up to the cabin, he saw that there were no other tracks in the new dusting of snow. His spirits buoyed. Maybe he would just wait around and see if Gillian showed up. It was a great place to hide out, especially this time of year.

He knew her. If she thought the ledger might be hidden at the cabin, she wouldn't tell the police. She would come for it herself. This cabin meant too much to her to have the police tearing the place apart looking for the ledger and any other evidence they thought they might find.

Even if the Texas deputy was still with Gillian this morning, it would just be the two of them. Marc hoped he was right. He'd brought several guns, including a rifle. This cabin that meant so much to his wife would be the perfect place to dispose of Gillian and the cowboy.

THE CABIN WAS back in the mountains that overlooked Canyon Ferry Lake. Huge green ponderosa pines glistened in the midday sun among large rock formations. It had snowed the night before but had now melted in all but the shade of the pines.

"Turn here," Gillian said when the road became little more than a Jeep trail.

Austin noticed tracks where someone had been up the road. He figured Gillian had noticed them, too. It could have been anyone. But he was guessing it was Marc Stewart. As the structure came into view, he saw that the windows were shuttered. At first glance, it didn't appear anyone had been inside for a very long time.

But as he parked, Austin saw that the front door was open a few inches and there were fresh gouges in the wood where whoever had been here had broken in. The old cabin looked like the perfect place for a wounded fugitive to lay low for a while and heal. Even though there was no sign of a vehicle and the tracks indicated that whoever had been here had left, he wasn't taking any chances.

"Stay here," Austin said as he opened his door and pulled his weapon. Long dried pine needles covered the steps up to the worn wood of the small porch. There were footprints in the wet dirt, large, man-sized soles. Austin moved cautiously as he pushed open the door. It groaned open.

A stale, musty scent rushed out. Weapon ready, Austin stepped into the dim darkness. The cabin was small so it didn't take long to make sure it was empty. As he looked around the ransacked room, it was clear that Marc had been here. From the destruction, Austin was betting the man hadn't found what he was looking for, though.

In a small trash container in the bathroom, he found some bloody bandages. From the amount of blood, it appeared Marc had been wounded enough to warrant medical attention. But no doubt not by anyone at a hospital, where the gunshot wound would have had to be reported.

When he returned to the porch, he found Gillian sitting on the front step looking out at the lake in the distance.

"He was here, wasn't he?" she said. "Did he—"

"I don't think he found anything."

Gillian nodded.

"You don't use the cabin?" Austin asked as he looked at the amazing view.

"No. It stayed in the family, but after my grandfather died…well, it just wasn't the same."

He watched her take a deep breath of mountain air before letting it out slowly. "I haven't been here in nine years. I doubt my sister has either, but I continue to pay the taxes on it."

Austin didn't want to believe that Rebecca Stewart had just been babbling when she'd mentioned the cabin. She had to be passing on a message.

"Would you mind taking a look around and see if your sister might have left you anything inside that Marc missed? He made a mess."

She nodded and pushed to her feet. There were tears in her eyes as she entered the cabin and stopped just inside the door.

Austin gave her a moment. He tried to imagine what it must have been like to visit here when Gillian's grandfather was alive. He and his brothers would have loved this place. Even at his age, he loved the smell of the pine trees, the crunch of the dried needles beneath his boot heels, the feeling of being a boy again in a place where there were huge rocks and trees to climb, forts to build and fish to catch out of the small stream that ran beside the cabin.

At the sound of her footfalls deeper in the cabin, he went inside to find her standing in the small kitchen. "My grandfather liked to cook. He made us pancakes." She looked over at Austin. "You remind me of him."

He couldn't help being touched by that. "Thank you."

Dust motes danced in the sunlight that streamed in through the cracks of the shutters. The interior of the cabin looked as if it might have been decorated in the 1950s or early 1960s. While rustic, it was cozy from the worn quilts on the couch and chairs to the soot-covered fireplace.

"There's nothing here." She shook her head. "Becky hasn't been here. She would have left at least a glass or two in the sink and an unmade bed. Everything is just as it was the last time I was here—except for the mess Marc made searching the place."

Austin couldn't help his disappointment. He'd hoped Rebecca had mentioned the cabin for a reason. Maybe she *had* been out of her head. As much as he wanted to find this ledger that would nail Marc Stewart to the wall, his greatest fear was for the boy. With whom would a woman possibly not in her right mind have stashed her ten-month-old son?

MARC HAD WAITED after he'd searched the cabin looking for the ledger. It wasn't there. He'd looked everywhere. He'd thought that maybe if Gillian really hadn't known what her sister had done with it that she and the cowboy might show up at the cabin.

But he'd never been good at waiting. Still, even as he was leaving, he hadn't been able to shake the feeling that Rebecca *had* been there. Had she left some message that he hadn't recognized? Frankly, he'd never thought his wife as that clever. But then again, he'd been wrong about how strong she was.

Belatedly, he was realizing that he might not have really known his wife at all.

RAW WITH EMOTIONS, Gillian looked around the cabin for a moment longer before turning toward the front door to escape even more painful memories.

She stumbled down the porch steps, breathing hard. Even the pine-scented air seemed to hurt her lungs. It, too, filled her with bittersweet memories.

Behind her, she heard Austin locking up the cabin. She felt as if she was going to be sick and stumbled down to the fallen tree her sister had reminded her about. Why hadn't Becky left her a clue? She'd wanted Gillian to find the ledger, get Marc put away and take care of Andy. But how did she expect her to do that without some idea of where to start? What had Becky been thinking?

She prayed that her sister had left Andy somewhere safe until she could find him.

"Is this the tree that blew over?" Austin said behind her, startling her.

Gillian stood leaning against it. The pine was old and huge. It had fallen during a summer thunderstorm, landing on a large boulder instead of falling all the way to the ground. Because of that, it laid at a slight slant a good three to six feet off the ground. She and her sister used to walk the length of it, pretending they were high-wire artists. Gillian had a scar on her arm from a fall she'd taken.

She told Austin about the night the tree fell and how she and Becky had played on it, needing to share the memories, fearing they would vanish otherwise. "It made a tremendous sound when it crashed," she said, her voice breaking.

"I was thinking earlier how my brothers and I would have loved this place."

She watched Austin walk around the root end of the tree. Most of the dirt that had once clung to the roots had washed off over the years in other storms. But because of its size, when the tree had become uprooted, it had left a large hole in the earth that she and Becky used to hide in.

"Gillian."

Something in the way he said her name made her start. She looked at his expression and felt a jolt. He was staring down into the hole.

"I think you'd better see this."

Chapter Seventeen

Austin stood back as Gillian hurried around the tree to the exposed roots and looked down into the deep cave of a hole. "What is that?"

She made a sound, half laugh, half sob. "That's Edgar."

"Edgar?" he repeated as she clambered down into the hole. She picked up what appeared to be a taxidermy-type stuffed crow on a small wooden stand and handed it up to him before he helped her out.

The bird had seen better days, but its dark eyes still glittered eerily. She took the mounted crow from him and began to cry as she held the bird to her as if it were a baby. "Edgar Allan Poe. Becky and I made friends with Edgar when he was young and orphaned. We fed him and kept him alive and he never left. He would fly in the moment we arrived at the cabin and caw at us from the porch railing. He followed us everywhere," she said excitedly and then sobered. "One time we came up and we didn't see him. We looked around for him…and found him dead. It was our grandfather's idea to have him mounted. Edgar had always looked out for us, Grandpa said. No reason he couldn't continue doing that."

Austin thought of the odd pets he and his brothers had accumulated and lost over the years and the attachment they'd had with them. "Your grandfather was a wise man."

She nodded through her tears. "Becky and I took Edgar to our tree house so he could keep an eye out for trespassers."

"Your tree house? Is that where you left him?"

Gillian met his gaze, hers widening. "Becky put Edgar here. That's what she was trying to tell me…" She pushed to her feet. "She *did* leave a message, since the last time I saw Edgar he was still in the tree house standing guard."

"Did Marc know about it?"

Gillian frowned. "I doubt it. He didn't like the outdoors much and his family's cabin was so much nicer on the lake in Idaho. Also I'm not sure how much of the tree house is even still there. It's been years."

Austin followed Gillian into the woods. They wound through the tall thick ponderosa pines. The December day was cold but clear. Sunlight slanted in through the trees but did little to warm them. The skiff of snow that had fallen overnight still hung to the pine boughs back here, making it feel even colder.

As they walked, he watched the ground for any sign that Marc had come this way. It was hard to tell since the ground was covered with pine needles.

They had gone quite a ways when Gillian stopped abruptly. He looked past her and saw what was left of the tree house. It was now little more than a few boards tacked up between trees. The years hadn't been kind to it. What boards had remained were weathered, several hanging by a nail.

He could feel Gillian's disappointment as they moved closer, stepping over the boards that had blown down. A makeshift ladder had been tacked to a tree at the base of what was left of the tree house. Austin tested the bottom step.

"I don't think it's safe for you to go up there," Gillian said.

"Your sister must have climbed up there." But he knew Rebecca weighed a lot less than he did as he tried the second step. The board held so he began the ascent, hoping for the best. It had been years since he'd climbed a tree. He'd forgotten the exhilaration of being high above the ground.

When he reached what was left of the tree house, he poked his head through the opening and felt a start much like he had when he'd seen Edgar down in the roots of the fallen tree.

"Do you see anything?" Gillian called up.

A fabric doll with curly dark hair sat in the corner of the remaining tree house floor, its back against the tree. It had huge dark eyes much like Gillian's and it was looking right at him. As he reached for it, he felt the soft material of the doll's yellow dress and knew it hadn't been in this tree long.

Other than the doll, there was nothing else in what had once been Gillian and Rebecca's tree house. He stuck the doll inside his coat and began the careful descent to the ground.

GILLIAN SET EDGAR down next to the base of a tree, thinking about her sister. Rebecca had always liked puzzles and scavenger hunts. This was definitely feeling like a combination of both.

As Austin pulled the doll from his coat, she stared at it in surprise for only a moment before taking it and crushing it to her chest in a hug.

"The doll looks like you," Austin said.

She nodded, afraid if she spoke she would burst into tears again. Her emotions were dangerously close to the surface as it was. Being here had brought back so many memories of the summers she and Becky had spent here with their grandfather.

After a moment, she held the doll at arm's length. The dolls had been a gift from their parents, she told Austin. "Mother had a woman make them so they resembled Becky and me. We never told her, but I found them to be a little creepy and used to turn mine against the wall when I slept. I half expected the doll to be turned around watching me when I woke up. But Becky loved hers so much she even took it when she went to college." That memory caused a hitch in her chest.

"The doll has to be a clue," Austin said.

"If it is, I have no idea what that clue might be." She studied the doll. Its dress was yellow, Gillian's favorite color, so she knew it was hers. The dress had tiny white rickrack around the collar and hem and puffy sleeves. She looked under the hem, thinking Becky might have left a note. Nothing. She felt all over the doll, praying for a scrap of paper, something sewn inside the stuffing, anything that would provide her with the information she desperately needed. Nothing.

When she looked at Austin, she felt her eyes tear up again. "I have no idea what this means, if anything."

"The doll wasn't in the tree long. Since it seems likely your sister left it there, it has to mean something."

She almost laughed. "If my sister was thinking clearly she wouldn't have climbed up into that tree to put my doll there without a note or some message…"

"Your sister was terrified that Marc would find not only the ledger but their son, right?" Austin asked.

She nodded.

"I know all this seems…illogical, but I think she knew she had to use clues that only you would understand, like Edgar."

"I hope you're right," she said, smiling at this man who'd been there for her since that first horrible night in the blizzard.

"Are you leaving Edgar here?" he asked.

Gillian nodded. "Becky always said this was his favorite spot. He used to fly around, landing on limbs near the tree house, watching over us as we played. I know it sounds silly—"

"No, it doesn't. I get it."

She saw that he did and felt her heart lift a little.

"So there were two dolls?" he asked. "Where is your sister's?"

Victor straightened the white clerical collar and checked himself in the mirror before picking up his Bible and exiting the car in the hospital parking lot.

He couldn't be sure how much security the cops had on Rebecca Stewart. He suspected it would be minimal. Most police departments were stretched thin as it was. This was Montana. Security at the hospital was seldom needed. Victor was counting on the uniform outside her room being some mall-type security cop that the hospital had brought in.

The security guard would have been given Marc Stewart's description, so the man would be on the lookout for him—not a pastor. The guard would have been on the job long enough that he would be bored and sick of hospital food.

As he walked into the lower entrance to the hospital, he saw that his "assistant" was already here sitting in one of the chairs in the lobby thumbing through a magazine.

He gave Candy only a cursory glance before he walked past the volunteer working at the desk.

While some hospitals were strict about visitors, this wasn't one of them. That's what he loved about small Montana communities. People felt safe.

He already knew the floor and room number and had asked about visiting hours, so he merely tipped his head at her and said, "Hope you're having a blessed day."

She smiled at him. "You, too, Reverend."

At the elevator, he punched in the floor number. A man and woman in lab coats hurried in. Victor gave them both a solemn nod and looked down at the Bible in his hands. Before the doors could close, a freshly manicured hand slipped between them. He caught the flash of bright red nail polish and the sweet scent of perfume.

As the doors were forced open, Candy stepped in, turning her back to the three of them.

He had told her to dress provocatively but not over the top. She'd chosen a conservative white blouse and slim navy skirt with a pair of strappy high heeled winter boots. The white blouse was unbuttoned enough that anyone looking got teasing glimpses of the tops of her full breasts. She smelled good, that, too, not overdone. Her blond hair was pulled up, a few strands curling around her pretty face.

Victor was pleased as the elevator stopped and the doors opened. They all stepped off, the man and woman in the lab coats scurrying down one hallway while he and Candy took the other. He let her get a few yards ahead before following. The way she moved reminded him of something from his childhood.

If I had a swing like that, I'd paint it red and put it in my backyard.

It was a silly thing to come to mind right now. He

worried that he was nervous and that it would tip off even the worst of security guards. So much was riding on this. If he could just get into Marc's wife's room…

At the end of the hallway, he spotted the rent-a-cop sitting in a plastic chair outside Rebecca Stewart's room.

The security guard spotted Candy and got to his feet as she approached.

Chapter Eighteen

Austin found himself watching his rearview mirror. If he was right, Rebecca Stewart had left a series of clues that only her sister could decipher. She'd used items from their past, the shared memories of sisters and things that even if she had mentioned to Marc, he wouldn't have recalled. It told Austin that she'd been terrified of her husband finding their son.

He could see that it was breaking Gillian's heart, these trips down memory lane with her sister. Had Rebecca worried that she could be dead by the time Gillian uncovered them? He figured she must have known her husband well enough that it had definitely been a consideration.

No wonder she hadn't told her sister a thing. Gillian would have done anything to save her sister and Marc would have known that. He must have realized Gillian didn't know the truth. Not that he hadn't planned to use her to try to get her sister to talk. There was no doubt in Austin's mind that, in an attempt to save her sister, Rebecca had pushed Marc and his rotten temper so he would lose control and kill her. If Gillian hadn't thrown herself at Marc when she had...

The drive north to Chinook took the rest of the day. They traveled from the Little Belt Mountains to the edge of the Rockies, before turning east across the wild praiie of Montana. It was dark by the time they reached the small Western town on what was known as the Hi-Line.

Chinook, like most of the towns along Highway 2, had sprung up with the introduction of the railroad. Both freight and passenger trains still blew their whistles as they passed through town.

A freight train rumbled past as Austin parked in front of a motor inn. Gillian had called ahead but had gotten no answer at the Baker house. Austin could tell that made her as nervous as it did him. Was it possible that as careful as Rebecca had been, Marc had been one step ahead of them?

"I can't believe Rebecca would have confided in anyone," Gillian said. "But if there is even a chance Nancy knows where Becky left Andy..."

Gillian had explained about her sister's doll on the drive north. Nancy Rexroth Baker and her sister had been roommates at college. Becky had been Nancy's maid of honor when she'd married Claude. While as far as Gillian knew the two hadn't stayed in touch when Nancy had a baby girl last year they'd named her Rebecca Jane. That's the name Nancy and Becky used to call her doll at college. Touched by this, her sister had mailed Nancy her doll.

"She told you this?" Austin had asked. "Wouldn't Marc have known?"

She shook her head. "Since my sister has apparently had this plot of hers in the works for some time, I wouldn't think so. But Marc is anything if not clever. He could have known a whole lot more than Becky suspected."

Gillian tried the Baker home number again. The line went to voice mail after four rings. "Maybe we should drive by the house."

Austin didn't think it would do much good, but he agreed. She gave him the address, which turned out to be in the older section of the town just four blocks from the motel. The houses were large with wide front porches, a lot of columns and arches.

The Baker house sat up on the side of a hill with a flight of stairs that ended at the wide white front porch. There were no lights on behind the large windows at the front, no Christmas decorations on the outside, and the drapes were drawn.

"Let's see if there is an alley," Austin said and drove around the corner. Just as he'd suspected, there was. He took it, driving down three houses before stopping in front of a garage. "I'll take a look." He hopped out to check the garage. As he peered in the window, he saw that it was empty.

It came as somewhat of a relief. As he climbed back into the SUV, he said, "It looks like they've gone somewhere for Christmas."

"Christmas." The way she said it made him think that she'd forgotten about it, just as he had, even with all the red and green lights strung around town.

He thought of his brothers all gathered in Big Sky for the holidays, no doubt wondering where he was. He quickly pushed the thought away. They should be used to him by now. Anyway, his cousin Dana would have told them he was tied up. Her husband, Hud, the marshal, would have a pretty good idea why he was tied up since he would have heard about Marc Stewart's attempted murder of his wife, the kidnapping of his sister-in-law, Gillian, and the BOLO out on Marc.

As Austin drove them back to the motel, he said, "We need to get into that house because if I'm right, then this family has your nephew and he's safe. The doll brought us this far. There has to be another clue that we're missing."

"The key," Gillian said on an excited breath. "The one I found at the house after Rebecca and Andy left. Do you still have it?"

"I'M GOING TO walk back and get into the house," Austin said after they returned to the motel. He'd gotten them adjoining rooms, no doubt so he could keep an eye on her, Gillian thought.

She was grateful for everything he'd done. But she was going with him. She came out of her room and stood in front of him, her hands on her hips. "You're not going alone."

He shook his head. "Maybe you don't understand the fine line between snooping and jail. Breaking and entering is—"

"I'm going with you."

He looked like he wanted to argue, but saw that she meant what she said. "Wear something dark and warm. It's cold out."

She was already one step ahead of him as she reached for a black fleece jacket she'd grabbed as they were leaving her apartment. Donning a hat and gloves, she turned to look at him.

He was smiling at her as if amused.

"What?" she said, suddenly feeling uncomfortable under his scrutiny. She knew it was silly. He'd seen her at her absolute worst.

"You just look so...cute," he said. "Clearly breaking the law excites you."

She smiled in spite of herself. It had been a while since a man had complimented her. Actually, way too long. But it wasn't breaking the law that excited her, she thought and felt her face heat with the thought.

The night was clear and cold, the sky ablaze with stars. She breathed in the freezing air. It stung her lungs, but made her feel more alive than she had in years. Fear drove her steps along with hope. The bird, the doll, all of it had led them here. She couldn't be wrong about this. And yet at the back of her mind, she worried that none of this made any sense because Rebecca hadn't known what she was doing.

At the dark alley, Austin slowed. It was late enough that there were lights on in the houses. Most of the drapes were open. She saw women in the kitchen cooking and families moving around inside the warm-looking homes. The scenes pulled at her, making her wish she and her sister were those women.

A few doors down, a dog barked, a door slammed and she heard someone calling, "Zoey!" The dog barked a couple more times; then the door slammed again and the alley grew quiet.

"Come on," Austin said and they started to turn down the alley.

A vehicle came around the corner, moving slowly. Gillian felt the headlights wash over them and let out a worried sound as she froze in midstep. Her first thought was Marc. Her heart began to pound even though she knew Austin had his shoulder holster on and the gun inside it was loaded.

Her moment of panic didn't subside when she saw that it was a sheriff's department vehicle.

"Austin?" she whispered, not sure what to do.

He turned to her and pulled her into his arms. Her mouth opened in surprise and the next thing she knew, he was kissing her. His mouth was warm against hers.

At first, she was too stunned to react. But after a moment, she put her arms around his neck and lost herself in the kiss.

As the headlights of the sheriff's car washed over them, the golden glow seemed to warm the night because she no longer felt cold. She let out a small helpless moan as Austin deepened the kiss, drawing her even closer.

As the sheriff's car went on past, she felt a pang of regret. Slowly, Austin drew back a little. His gaze locked with hers, and for a moment they stood like that, their quickened warm breaths coming out in white clouds.

"Sorry."

She shook her head. She wasn't sorry. She felt…lightheaded, happy, as if helium filled. She thought she might drift off into the night if he let go of her.

"Are you okay?" he asked, looking worried.

She unconsciously touched the tip of her tongue to her lower lip, then bit down on it to stop herself. "Great. Never better."

That made him smile. For a moment, he stood merely smiling at her, his gaze on hers, his dark eyes as warm as a crackling fire. Then he sighed. "Let's get this over with," he said and took her gloved hand as they started up the alley.

There was only an inch of snow on the ground, but it crunched under their feet. If anyone heard them and looked out their window, she doubted they would think anything of it. They would appear to be what they were, a thirtysomething couple out walking on an early December night.

She looked over at Austin. Light from one of the yards shone on his handsome face, catching her off guard. He wasn't just handsome. He was caring and kind and capable, as well. She warned herself not to let one kiss go to her head. Of course she felt something for this man who'd saved her life twice and probably would have to again before this was over.

But her pulse was still pounding hard from the kiss. It had been the best kiss she'd ever had. Not that it meant anything.

She reminded herself that this was what Austin Cardwell did for a living. Not kiss women he was trying to save, but definitely doing whatever it took to save those same women.

She'd bet there was a long line of women he'd saved and all of them had gone giddy if he'd kissed them like that. That was a sobering thought. He could have ended up kissing all of them. Or even something more intimate.

That thought settled her down. She was behaving like a teenager on a date with the adorable quarterback of the football team. She told herself it was only because she hadn't dated all that much, especially since she'd started her business. True, she hadn't met anyone she cared to date. But she wasn't the kind of woman who fell head over heels at the drop of a kiss. Even one amazing kiss on a cold winter night.

But any woman in her place would be feeling like this, she told herself. She'd never believed that knights on white horses really existed before Austin Cardwell. It was one reason she was still single. That and she liked her independence. But mostly, it was because she'd never met a man who had ever made her even consider marriage.

Becky's marriage to Marc certainly hadn't changed her mind about men in general. She'd known Marc was domineering. She just hadn't known what the man was capable of. She doubted Becky had either.

Just the thought of her sister brought tears to her eyes. She wiped at them with her free gloved hand, determined not to break down, especially now. Austin hadn't wanted to bring her along as it was.

She needed to be strong. She concentrated on finding Andy. Becky had hidden him somewhere safe. Gillian had to believe that. What better place than with someone she could trust, like her former college roommate, Nancy Baker?

Gillian hated that she'd let Marc keep her from her sister. But the few times she'd visited he'd made her so uncomfortable that she hadn't gone back. And Marc had put Becky on a leash that didn't allow her to come up to Big Sky to visit often. It wasn't that he forbade it, he just made sure Becky was too busy to go anywhere.

Rubbing a hand over her face, she tried to concentrate on what lay ahead rather than wallowing in regret. Becky was stable. Gillian couldn't count on her regaining consciousness. It was why she had to find Andy—and that damned ledger before Marc did.

Austin slowed as they reached the back of the Baker house. She saw him look down the alley both ways before he drew her into the shadows along the side of the garage. The yard stretched before them. Huge pines grew along the sides against a tall wooden fence.

They walked toward the back of the house staying in the deep cold shadows of the pines. At the back door, Austin hesitated for a moment. She could tell he was listening. She heard voices but in the distance. Someone was calling a child into the house for dinner. Closer, that same dog barked.

Austin headed up the steps to the back door. She followed trying to be as quiet as possible. The houses weren't particularly close, but this was a small town. Neighbors kept an eye on each other's homes, especially when they knew a family was away for Christmas.

That was where the Bakers had gone, wasn't it?

Gillian took a deep breath as she saw Austin pull out the key. It was such a long shot, she realized now, that she felt silly even mentioning it. But it didn't matter if the key worked or not. She knew Austin would get them into the house. She was praying once they got in the house that they wouldn't find evidence of Marc having been there—and especially not of any kind of struggle.

She held her breath as he tried the key. It slipped right in. Austin shot her a look, then turned the key. She felt her eyes widen as the door opened.

"Rebecca left the key," she said more to herself than to Austin. She knew she sounded as disbelieving as he must have felt. Her heart lifted with the first feeling of real hope she'd felt since Marc had abducted her. "It has to mean that Nancy has my nephew, that Andy is safe."

As CANDY APPROACHED, the security guard ran a hand down the front of his uniform as if to get out any wrinkles and remind himself to suck in his stomach. He stood a little straighter as well, puffing up a bit, without even realizing he was doing it, Victor thought amused.

"May I help you?" the guard asked her.

Candy gave him one of her disarming smiles.

Victor saw that it was working like a charm. He looked into one of the rooms, before moving down the hall to Rebecca's. He could hear Candy asking for directions, explaining that her best friend had just had her third baby.

"Ten pounds, eleven ounces! I can't even imagine."

Victor smiled and gave a somber nod to the guard as he pushed open the door to Rebecca's room. He was so close, he could almost taste it.

"Just a minute," the guard said, stopping him.

"I told the family I would look in on Mrs. Stewart," Victor said.

"Did you say first floor like down by the cafeteria?" Candy asked the guard, then dropped her purse. It fell open. Coins tinkled on the floor. A lipstick rolled to the guard's feet.

The guard began to stoop down to help pick it up, but shot Victor another look before waving him in.

"I'm so sorry," Candy was saying as the door closed behind Victor. "I'm so clumsy. How did you say I get to my friend's room? I would have sworn she said it was on this floor."

Victor approached the bed. He'd met Marc's wife only once and that had been by accident. He liked to keep his business and personal lives entirely separate. But there'd been a foul-up in a shipment so he'd stopped by Marc's auto shop one night after hours. Marc had told him he would be there so he hadn't been surprised to see a light burning in the rear office.

As he'd pushed open the side door, though, he'd come face-to-face with a very pregnant and pretty dark-haired woman. She'd had a scowl on her face and he could see that she'd been crying. It hadn't taken much of a leap to know she must be Marc's wife. Or mistress.

"Sorry," she'd said, sounding breathless.

He'd realized that he'd startled her. *"I'm the one who's sorry."*

"Are you here to see Marc?"

"I left my car earlier," Victor had ad-libbed. *"The owner said he might have it finished later tonight. I saw the light on...."*

She'd nodded, clearly no longer interested. *"He's in his office,"* she'd said and he'd moved aside to let her leave.

As the door closed behind her, Marc had come out

of his office looking sheepish. *"I didn't know she was stopping by."* He'd shrugged. *"My wife. She's pregnant and impossible. I'll be so glad when this baby is finally born. Maybe she will get off my ass."*

Victor hadn't cared about Marc's marital problems. He'd never guessed that night that Rebecca Stewart might someday try to take them all down in one fell swoop.

As he stepped to the side of the bed and looked down at the woman lying there, he could see the brutality Marc had unleashed on her. His hands balled into fists at his side. He'd known this kind of violence firsthand and had spent a lifetime trying to overcome it in himself.

"Rebecca?"

Not even the flicker of an eyelid.

"Rebecca?" he said, leaning closer. "How are you doing today?"

Still nothing. Glancing toward the door, he could hear Candy just outside the room, still monopolizing the guard's attention.

Victor pulled the syringe from his pocket. He couldn't let this woman wake up and tell the police where they could find the ledger. He uncapped the syringe and reached for the IV tube.

Rebecca's eyes flew open before he could administer the drug. She let out a sound just a moment before the alarm on the machine next to her went off.

Chapter Nineteen

Marc could feel time slipping through his fingers like water. He tried to remain calm, to think. With a start, he realized something. If Gillian knew where the ledger and Andy were, then she would go to both. Once she had the ledger in her hot little hands, she would turn it over to the cops. Victor would be on his private jet, winging his way out of the country—after he had Marc killed.

Which meant Gillian really didn't know where either item was. It was the only thing that made any sense because otherwise, by now, the ledger would be in the hands of the police.

But she would be looking for it. Was she stumbling around in the dark like he was? Or had her sister given her a hint where it was? Unlike her, he had cops after him. He felt as if he was waiting for the other shoe to drop. Once that ledger surfaced... He didn't want to think about how much worse things could get for him.

For a moment, he almost wished that Rebecca had cut his throat and he'd died right there at her feet—after he'd pulled the trigger and put the both of them out of their misery.

Marc shook himself out of those dark thoughts. If he was right and Gillian didn't have a clue where the ledger was any more than he did…well, then there was still hope. He dug out his cell phone.

When the hospital answered, he asked about Rebecca's condition.

"I'm sorry," the nurse said. "I can't give out that information."

"There must be someone I can talk to. I'm her brother. I can't fly out until later in the week. I'm afraid it will be too late."

"Let me connect you to her floor."

He waited. A male nurse came on the line. He could hear noise in the background. Something was happening. Was it Rebecca?

When he asked about his "sister's" condition, the nurse started to say he couldn't give out that information over the phone. "How about her doctor? Surely I can talk to someone there." He gave him his hard-luck pitch about not being able to get there right away.

"Perhaps you'd like to talk to the pastor who just went into her room," the nurse said.

Pastor? Marc stifled a curse. *Victor.* That son of a…

"I'm sorry, I don't see him," the nurse said. "Why don't I have the doctor call you?"

Marc slammed down the phone and let out a string of oaths. How dare Victor. Marc had told him he'd handle this. Not only that, he wanted to be the person who killed her—after he found out where she'd hidden the ledger and his son.

So was Rebecca dead? The last person Victor had paid a visit to while dressed as a pastor…well, needless to say, that person had taken a turn for the worst.

ONCE THE DOOR of the Baker house closed behind them, Austin snapped on his small penlight and handed a second one to Gillian. The silence inside the house gave him the impression that no one had been home for some time.

They were standing in the kitchen. He swung the light over the counter. Empty. Everything was immaculate. No dishes in the sink. Stepping to the refrigerator, he opened it. There was nothing but condiments. No leftovers that would spoil while the family was gone. As he closed the door, he noticed the photographs tacked to it and the children's artwork. There was no photo of Gillian's sister.

"They're gone, aren't they?" Gillian said from the doorway to the living room. "But they must have Andy. My sister wouldn't have left me the key unless..." She stopped to look at him in the dim light.

He agreed, but he knew they both wanted proof. "Let's check the kid's room upstairs." It made sense that if this family had Andy they might have left something behind to assure Gillian that her nephew was fine, or, better yet, another clue as to where Gillian could find the ledger and put Marc away for a long time.

As they moved through the living room, Gillian whispered, "No Christmas tree. No presents. They aren't coming back until after Christmas."

Or until they hear that it's safe, he thought. Had Rebecca told them she would call them when it was safe? But what if she couldn't call?

They climbed the stairs to the bedrooms. It didn't take long to find the child's room. It was bright colored with stuffed animals piled on the bed. Gillian stepped to the bed. He knew she must be looking for her sister's doll. It wasn't there.

"Do you see anything of Andy's?" he asked.

She sighed and shook her head. "His favorite toy is a plush owl, but it's not here. Then again, it wouldn't be.

He'd want it with him, especially if he wasn't with his mother." Her voice broke.

They checked the other rooms but found nothing. Going back downstairs, Austin looked more closely in the living room. Rebecca had been scared of her husband. But her clues for Gillian did make him wonder about the state of her mind. He reminded himself that she'd been terrified of Marc. The clues had to be vague, things only Gillian would understand.

They searched the house, but found nothing that would indicate that Andy Stewart had been here. Like Gillian, he kept telling himself that Rebecca had left them a key to this house. Didn't that mean that the Bakers had Andy and all were safe since there was no sign of a struggle in the house?

He'd stopped to go through a desk in the study when he heard Gillian go into the kitchen. She had looked as despondent as he felt. He'd been so sure they would find—

Gillian let out a cry. Austin rushed into the kitchen to find her standing in front of the refrigerator. Her hand was covering her mouth and her eyes were full of tears as her penlight glared off the refrigerator door.

He'd checked the kitchen first thing and hadn't seen anything. As he moved closer, she pointed at what he'd assumed had been artwork done by the daughter. What he hadn't seen was a note of any kind.

"What?" he asked, looking from Gillian to the front of the refrigerator in confusion.

She carefully plucked one of the pieces of artwork from the door. "Andy."

He looked down at the sheet of paper in her hand. It was a drawing of an owl with huge round eyes. Someone had taken a crayon to it. The owl was almost indistinguishable under the purple scribbles.

"Andy?" he repeated confused.

"I told you. He loves owls."

That seemed a leap even to him.

Gillian began to laugh. "Rebecca drew this at my house when she and Andy came up to visit. Andy's favorite color is purple."

"You're sure this is the same drawing?" he asked. He couldn't help being skeptical.

"Positive. Look at this." She pointed to a spot on the owl. The artist had drawn in feathers before they had been scribbled over. In the feathers he saw what appeared to be numbers. "It's a phone number. I'm betting it is Nancy Baker's cell phone number."

VICTOR POCKETED THE syringe as he stepped back from the hospital bed. Rebecca Stewart's eyes were open. She was staring right at him, a wild, frightened look in her dark eyes.

As a doctor and two nurses rushed in, the security guard at their heels, Victor clutched his Bible and moved aside.

"What happened?" the doctor demanded.

"Nothing," he said. "That is, I was saying a prayer over her when she suddenly opened her eyes and that alarm went off."

The doctor began barking orders to the nurses. "If you don't mind stepping out, Pastor."

"I have other patients I promised to see, but I will check back before I leave," Victor said, but the doctor was busy and didn't seem to care.

On the overhead intercom, a nurse was calling a code blue as he walked toward the door. He felt the security guard's gaze on him as he stepped aside to let a crash cart be wheeled into the room. Without looking at the man, Victor started down the hallway away from all the noise and commotion in Rebecca's hospital room.

He half expected the security guard to call after him, but when he glanced back as he ducked into the first restroom he came to he saw that the guard was more interested in what was going on in Rebecca's room.

Reaching into his pocket he put on the latex gloves, then carefully removed the syringe from his other pocket and stuffed it down into the trash. Removing the gloves, he discarded them, as well. After washing his hands, he left.

The security guard didn't look his way as Victor turned and walked down the hallway, stopping at one of the empty rooms for a moment as if visiting a patient.

The guard hadn't asked his name. No one had. As he left the empty room, he saw a nurse coming out of Rebecca's room with the crash cart. He couldn't tell by the woman's face what the outcome had been for the patient.

Nor did he dare wait to find out. Turning, he walked out of the hospital.

Chapter Twenty

Marc felt sick to his stomach. His fingers shook as he dialed the hospital. Again, he pretended to be her brother.

"I have to know her condition. I can't get a flight out because of the weather right now. Tell me I'm not going to get there too late."

"Just a moment. Let me check," the nurse finally said, relenting.

He waited, his heart pounding. As long as Rebecca was alive, he stood a chance of fixing this mess. He would do anything she wanted. He would convince her to give up the ledger to save not just her own life but his and their son's. She had no idea the kind of people who would be after her and Andy.

But if Victor had killed her... *Hell,* he thought. The cops would think he'd done it! Or paid someone to do it. What had Victor been thinking?

The answer came to him like another blow, this one more painful than the crystal tumbler. Victor planned to kill everyone who knew about the ledger and what was in it. He would take his chances that wherever Rebecca had hidden it, the incriminating book wouldn't turn up. Or if it did, the finder wouldn't have a clue what it was and wouldn't take it to the authorities. Or...it was this third option that made his pulse jump. Or…Victor was tying up loose ends before he skipped the country.

The nurse came back on the line. Marc held his breath.

"Good news. Your sister's condition has been upgraded. She had an episode earlier, but the doctor is cautiously optimistic about her complete recovery."

He tried to breathe. Victor had failed? His relief was real. "Can I talk to her?"

"I'm afraid not. The doctor wants her to rest. She is drifting in and out of consciousness. Perhaps by tomorrow…"

GILLIAN COULDN'T BEAR to wait until they returned to the motel to make the call, but Austin was anxious to get out of the house. She tried the number she'd found on Rebecca and Andy's artwork on the walk back to the motel.

The phone was answered on the second ring. "Gillian?"

"Nancy." She began to cry.

"Is everything all right?" Nancy asked, sounding as anxious as Gillian felt.

"I'm sorry, I'm just so relieved. Tell me you have Andy."

Several heartbeats of unbearable silence before Nancy said, "He's safe."

"Thank God."

"He keeps asking about his mother, though. Rebecca said she would join us before Christmas."

Gillian didn't know how to tell her. "Rebecca's in the hospital. The last I heard, she's unconscious."

"Oh, no. And Marc?"

"He's on the loose. Tell me you have Andy somewhere Marc wouldn't dream of looking."

"We do."

"A deputy sheriff from Texas is helping me try to find a ledger that will send Marc to prison. Do you know anything about it?"

"No. Rebecca only told me that Marc was dangerous and she needed Andy to be safe until she could come get him. She doesn't even know where we are. I was to tell her only when she called."

"Good. I don't need to know either. I can't tell you how relieved I am that Andy is with you and safe. But did Rebecca give you a message to pass on to me if I called?"

"She did mention that it was possible you would call."

So her sister had feared she wouldn't be able to call herself. Gillian felt sick.

"Becky said that if you called to tell you she forgives you for the birthday present you gave her when she turned fourteen and that she is overcoming her fears, just as you suggested. Does that make any sense to you?"

Gillian tried hard not to burst into uncontrollable sobs. "Yes, it does," she managed to say. "That's all?"

"That's it. Whatever is going on, it reminded me of how much your sister always loved puzzles."

"Yes. I'm just grateful that Andy is with you and safe. Give him my love."

She disconnected, still fighting tears. "Andy's safe."

"I heard. Your sister left you another clue?" he asked.

Before she could answer, she saw that she had a message. "The hospital called." She hurriedly returned the call, praying that it would be good news. *Please let Becky be all right. Please.*

"Yes," the floor nurse said when he finally came on the line. "We called you to let you know that your sister is doing much better. She has regained consciousness."

"Can I talk to her?"

"I'm sorry. The doctor gave her something for the pain. She's asleep. Maybe in the morning."

Gillian smiled through fresh tears as she disconnected. "Rebecca is better." She gulped the cold night air. "And I think I know where she hid the ledger."

MARC HUNG UP from his call to the hospital, still shocked that Victor had failed. Rebecca was alive. Didn't that mean he had a chance to reason with her? He knew it was a long shot that he could persuade Rebecca of anything at this point. But if she realized the magnitude of what she'd done, given the criminal nature of his associates, maybe she would do it for Andy's sake…

He wished he'd explained things in the first place instead of losing his temper. He thought of Victor, Mr. Cool, and began to laugh. Victor must be beside himself. He was a man who didn't like to fail.

Would he try to kill Rebecca again? Marc didn't think so. It would be too dangerous. He was surprised that Victor had decided to do the job himself. That, he realized, showed how concerned the man was about cleaning up this mess—and how little confidence Victor had in him.

I'm toast.

If he'd had any doubt that Victor wouldn't let him survive, he no longer did. Now he had only one choice. Save himself. To do that, it meant going to the feds. But without the ledger…he couldn't remember names and numbers. He'd been told he was dyslexic. But he knew that wasn't right because he'd heard dyslexics had trouble writing words and numbers correctly. He thought it had more to do with not being able to remember. He could write just fine. That's what had him in this trouble.

When Victor had asked him why he'd done something so stupid as to write everything down, Marc hadn't wanted to admit that there was anything wrong with him. He'd hired someone else to handle the details at his auto shop.

But he couldn't very well do that with the criminal side of his work, could he? He told himself it was too late to second-guess that decision. He had to get his hands on the ledger. He realized there was a second option besides turning it over to the feds. He could skip the country with it. The ledger would be his insurance against Victor dusting him.

Without the ledger, though, he had no bargaining power.

Sure he knew some things about Victor's operation, but not enough without the ledger. It contained the names and dates, names he knew the feds would love to get their hands on.

Rebecca! What did you do with that damned book?

It wasn't as if he hadn't been suspicious that she was up to something in the weeks before. He'd actually thought she might be having an affair. But he'd realized that was crazy. What would she have done with Andy? It wasn't like she had a friend to watch their son. No, he'd known it had to be something else.

He wondered if she'd taken up gambling. He didn't give her much money, but she had a way of stretching what he did… No, he'd ruled out gambling. Unless she won all the time, that didn't explain her disappearances.

He had started making a habit of calling home at different hours to check on her. She was never there. Oh, sure, she made excuses.

Andy and I were outside in the yard. I didn't hear the phone. Or she didn't have her cell phone on her. Other times she was at the park or the mall. She would say it must have been too noisy to hear her phone. He told her to put it on vibrate and stick the thing in her pocket.

"Was there something you wanted?" she'd asked.

He hadn't liked the tone of her voice. She'd seemed pretty uppity. Like a woman who knew something he didn't. He'd said, "I was just making sure you and Andy were all right. That's what husbands do."

"Really." She'd actually scoffed at that.

Not only had he resented her attitude, he'd also hated that she acted as if she was smarter than him. Or worse, that she thought for a moment that she could outwit him.

That's why he'd started writing down the mileage on her car.

He had checked it each night after that since he usually got in after she and the kid were asleep, and then he would compare it the next night. It had been a head-scratcher, though. She had never gone far, so while he'd continued to write it down, he hadn't paid any attention lately.

He fished out the scrap of paper he'd been writing it down on from his wallet and did a little math. At first he thought he'd read it wrong. She'd gone over a hundred miles four days ago. The day before she'd drugged him with his own drugs, stolen his ledger and hidden his son, she'd driven more than fifty miles that morning alone.

What the hell? Marc realized that he hadn't seen his son that day. Had she already hidden him away somewhere the day before? He tried to remember. He'd gotten home late that night. He glanced into his son's room. He hadn't actually seen the boy in his bed. It could have been the kid's pillow under the covers.

He let out a string of curses. Where had she gone? Not to her family cabin, he'd already checked it. Then where? He refused to let her outsmart him. He pulled a map of

Montana from the glove box. It was old, but it would do. Suddenly excited, he drew a circle encompassing twenty to twenty-five miles out from Helena. Rebecca thought she was so smart. He'd show her.

Chapter Twenty-One

"What do you want to do?" Laramie asked his brothers. They were all sitting around the large kitchen table at their cousin Dana Savage's house on Cardwell Ranch. They'd just finished a breakfast of flapjacks, ham, fried potatoes and eggs. Hud had motioned his wife to stay where she was as he got up to refill all of their mugs with coffee.

"I hate to put off the grand opening of the restaurant," Tag said.

"Can't it wait until Austin can be here?" Dana asked.

Jackson got up to check on the kids, who were eating at a small table in the dining room. "We might never have a grand opening if we do that."

"Jackson's right," his brother Hayes said. "We know how Austin is and now apparently he's gotten involved with some woman who's in trouble." He looked toward Hud for confirmation.

The marshal finished filling their cups and said, "He got involved in a situation where he was needed. That's all I can tell you."

"A dangerous situation?" Dana asked.

Hud didn't answer. He didn't have to. His brothers knew Austin, and Dana was married to a marshal. She knew how dangerous his line of work could be.

"This is the woman he met in the middle of the highway, right?" Laramie shook his head. "This is his M.O. He'd much rather be working than be with his family."

"I don't think that's true," Dana said in her cousin's defense. "I talked to him. He can't just abandon this woman. You should be proud that he's so dedicated. And as I recall, there are several of you who are into saving women in need." She grinned. "I believe it is why some of you are now married and others are involved in wedding planning."

There were some chuckles around the table.

Laramie sighed. "Some of us are still interested in the business that keeps us all fed, though. Fortunately," he added. "Let's go ahead with the January first grand opening. I, for one, will be glad to get back to Texas. I am freezing up here."

His brothers laughed, but agreed.

"Maybe Austin will surprise you," Dana said.

Laramie saw a look pass between Dana and her marshal husband. He was worried about Austin. Last July, Austin had been shot and had almost died trying to get some woman out of a bad situation. He just hoped this wouldn't prove to be as dangerous.

MARC WENT TO an out-of-the-way bar. He hadn't seen a tail, but that didn't mean there wasn't one again. In a quiet corner of the bar, he studied the map and tried to remember any places Rebecca might have mentioned. He had a habit of tuning her out. Now he wished he'd paid more attention.

They'd gone to a few places while they were dating, but he doubted she would be sentimental about any of them, the way things had turned out. He had never understood women, though, so maybe she would hide the ledger in one of those places because she thought it was a place he would never look.

Just trying to think like her gave him a headache. He wanted to choke the life out of the woman for putting him through this. He realized he hadn't heard from Victor demanding an update. Which he figured meant he was right about one of Victor's men tailing him again.

He'd lost the tail the first time, but maybe Victor had put someone like Jumbo on him. Jumbo was a more refined criminal, not all muscle and no brains, which made him very dangerous.

Marc folded the map and put it away. He couldn't do anything until daylight. Between songs on the jukebox, he put in another call to the hospital with his brother story. He knew he was whistling in the dark. He'd be lucky if he even got to talk to Rebecca, let alone convince her he was sorry. But it was a small hospital and he doubted the cops had done more than put security outside her room, if that, since Victor had circumvented whatever safety guards they'd taken.

Still to his amazement, he was put through to Rebecca's room.

"Hello?" she sounded weak but alive. "Hello?"

"Becky, listen," he said once he got past his initial shock. "Don't hang up. I have to tell you something."

Silence.

"Are you still there?" He hated that his voice broke and even more that she'd heard it.

"What could you possibly want, Marc?"

Humor. He bit back a nasty retort. "That book you took, it doesn't just implicate me. The people I work for… Rebecca they won't let you live if I don't get that book back."

"Don't you mean they won't let *you* live?"

"Not just me. They'll go after your sister, too." He could hear her breathing. "And Andy." His voice broke at the thought.

"You bastard, what have you gotten us all into?"

"Hey, if you had left well enough alone—"

"What is it? Drugs?"

"It doesn't matter what it is. I was only trying to make some money for Andy. I wanted him to have a better life than I had."

"Money for Andy? You are such a liar, Marc." She laughed. It was a weak laugh, but still it made his teeth hurt. "You hid that money for yourself."

And now she had a large portion of it. She'd hidden that, too, he reminded himself. He felt his blood pressure go through the roof. He still couldn't believe she'd done this to him. If he could have gotten his hands on her... He took a breath, trying to regain control, as he reminded himself that he needed her help.

"Rebecca, honey, you just didn't realize what you were getting in to. But we can fix this. I can save you and your sister and our son. These people...sweetie, I need to know what you did with the ledger. Did you mail it to the police?" Her hesitation gave him hope. "I know I reacted...badly. But, honey, I knew what would happen if that ledger got into the wrong hands. These people aren't going to stop. They will kill you. I suspect one of them has already tried. You didn't happen to see a man dressed as a pastor, did you?"

Her quick intake of breath told him she had "A blond guy, good looking. He was there to kill you."

She started to say something, but began coughing. He could hear how weak and sick she was.

"He isn't going to give up. The only way out of this is the ledger. I can save us both. Honey, I'm begging you."

"Begging me?" She sounded like she was crying. "You mean like I begged you for a divorce?"

"I'm sorry. I'll give you a divorce. I'll even give you custody of Andy. I'll give you whatever you want. Just tell me where the ledger is so I can make this right."

"I don't think so," she said, her voice stronger. "It's over, Marc. I never want to see you again. Once the police arrest you…"

He swore under his breath. "I'll get out of jail at some point, Rebecca."

"Not if I have my way." The line went dead. As dead as they were both going to be, because if he went, she was going with him one way or another.

"So she told you where we could find the ledger?" Austin asked as he and Gillian walked back to the motel. She'd grown quiet after the call. He wondered if this last clue was one she didn't want to share. Was she worried she couldn't trust him?

When she said nothing, he asked, "Is something wrong?"

She looked over at him, her dark eyes bright. "I'm glad you're here with me."

Her words touched him more than they should have. There was something about this woman… He smiled, his heart beating a little faster. "So am I," he said, taking her gloved hand.

As if the touch of her had done it, snow began to fall in thick, lacy flakes that instantly clung to their clothing.

Gillian laughed. It was a wonderful sound in the snowy night. "Andy is safe, my sister is going to be all right and Marc Stewart is going to get what's coming to him." She moved closer to him as they walked. "How do you feel about caves?"

"Caves?" he said, looking over at her in surprise.

"Assuming my sister was in her right mind, she hid the ledger in a cave." She repeated the so-called clue Nancy Baker had given her.

"And from that you've decided the ledger is in some cave?"

"Not just some cave. One up Miners Gulch near Canyon Ferry Lake. Rebecca is terrified of close places, especially caves. It's a boy's fault we ended up in one on her fourteenth birthday. I had this horrible crush on a boy named Luke Snider. He was a roughneck, wild and unruly, and adorable. I was sixteen and dreamed of the two of us on outrageous adventures. I thought I would see the world with him, live in exotic places, eat strange food and make love under a different moon every night."

They had almost reached the motel. He hated to go inside. The night had taken on a magical quality. Or maybe it was just sharing it with Gillian that made him feel that way.

"You were quite the romantic at sixteen."

She laughed. "I was, wasn't I? It didn't last any longer than my crush. Luke graduated from high school, went to work at his father's tire shop. He still works there. I bought a tire from him once." She smiled at that. "I definitely dodged a bullet with Luke."

He laughed as he let go of her hand and reached for the room key.

Gillian turned her face out toward the snow. He watched her breathe in the freezing air and let it out in a sigh. "If I'm right about this clue then my sister is getting even with me for being such a brat on her birthday that year." She seemed as reluctant as he did to leave the snow and the night behind, but stepped inside.

"I suspect caves have something to do with Luke and your sister's birthday," he said.

Gillian shook snowflakes from her coat. As she slipped out of it, he took it and hung her coat, along with his own, up to dry when she made no move to go into her adjoining room.

"I overheard Luke and his friends say they were going to these caves in the gulch. I knew they wouldn't let me go along, but if I just happened to run into them in the caves… I didn't want to go alone to look for them, and my friends could not imagine what I saw in Luke and his friends. You know how it is when you're sixteen. Just seeing him, saying hi in the hall, could make my day. I wanted him to really notice me. I figured if he saw how adventurous I was in the caves… So I told my sister I had a surprise birthday present for her."

He shook his head, smiling, remembering being sixteen and impulsive. He'd also had his share of teenage crushes. He hated to think of some of the things he'd done to impress a girl. He offered her the motel chair, anxious to hear her story, but she motioned it away and sat down on the end of his bed.

"Rebecca is claustrophobic so the last place she wanted to go was into a cave. I told her she needed to overcome her fears. Her message she left with Nancy was that she was now overcoming her fears."

"She mentioned this birthday present, so you think she put the ledger somewhere in these caves?"

"If I'm right, I know the exact spot." Gillian gave him a sad smile. "The spot where Rebecca totally freaked that day." Tears filled her eyes.

Austin reached across to take her hand. "Ah, child-hood memories. I can't even begin to tell you about all the terrible things my brothers and I did to each other. It's just what siblings do."

She shook her head. "I hate that I did that to her."

"And yet, when the chips were down, she went back into those caves with you."

She smiled. "If I'm right."

His voice softened. "You've been right so far about everything."

GILLIAN FELT A lump form in her throat. Her pulse buzzed at the look in his eyes. If he kissed her again... "I should—"

"Yes," he said, letting go of her. "We should get some sleep. Sounds like we have a big day ahead of us tomorrow." He rose and stepped back, looking uncertain as if he didn't seem to know what to do with his hands.

She thought of being in his arms and how easy it would be to find herself in his bed. She told herself she was feeling like this about him because he'd saved her life, but a part of her knew it was more than that. It was... chemistry? She almost laughed at the thought. It sounded so...high school.

But she couldn't deny how powerful it had felt when he'd kissed her. Or now, the way he'd looked at her with those dark eyes. She marveled at the feeling since it was something she hadn't felt in a long time. Nor had she ever experienced anything this intense. The air around them seemed to buzz with it.

He'd felt it, too. She'd seen it in his expression. What made her laugh was that she could tell he was even more afraid of whatever was happening between them than she was.

"Something funny?" he asked.

Gillian shook her head and took a step back in the

direction of her room. She realized she loved feeling like this. It didn't matter that it couldn't last. "Thank you again for *everything*."

He smiled at that and almost looked bashful.

"Everything," she repeated and stepped through the doorway, closing the adjoining door to lean against it. Her heart was pounding, her skin tingling and there was an ache inside her that made her feel silly and happy at the unexpected longing.

Chapter Twenty-Two

Marc spent the night in a crummy old motel. He couldn't go home. Not only were the cops looking for him but also he had Victor's enforcers on his tail. Victor had failed yesterday at the hospital. That meant he'd be in an even fouler mood. Marc hoped he wouldn't have to see him for a while. Never would be even better.

He'd fallen asleep after staring at the map for hours. His face hurt like hell, not to mention his shoulder. He'd drunk a pint of whiskey he'd picked up at the bar. It hadn't helped. He thought about changing the bandage, but wasn't up to looking at the damage this morning in the mirror.

Picking up the map, he stared again at the circle he'd drawn around Helena. Maybe he should expand it. That one day, she'd driven a hundred miles. He made another circle, this one fifty miles out around the city.

Where the hell did she go? He had no idea since he couldn't conceive of a place she might think to hide the ledger. She knew him and he'd thought he'd known her. She would have had to up her game to beat him, and she would have known that.

He thought back to the days before he'd awakened still half drugged and found her note telling him how things were going to be now.

Marc started to shake his head in frustration when he recalled coming home early one day to find Andy crying and Rebecca looking…looking guilty, he thought now. She'd been standing in the kitchen.

He'd told her to shut the kid up, which she had. Then she'd disappeared into the bedroom to change her clothes. He frowned now. Why had she needed to change her clothes? At the time, he couldn't have cared less. They hardly ever had sex except when he forced the issue. He hadn't been in the mood that day or he might have followed her into the bedroom and taken advantage of the situation.

What had she been wearing that she'd had to change? His pulse jumped and he sat up straighter as he imagined her standing *before* him—before she'd changed her clothing. She was wearing the pair of canvas pants he'd bought her for hunting. She'd only worn them once when she'd tagged along. It had been early in their marriage. He'd made the trip as miserable as he could since he had been hoping she wouldn't ask to come along again.

Why would she have been wearing such heavy-duty pants? He recalled that their knees had been soiled. And Rebecca's hair had been a mess. She'd looked as if she'd been working out in the yard. But there'd been snow on the ground. Where had she been that she'd gotten what had looked like mud on the pant knees?

He realized with a start that it must have been the same day she'd put so many miles on her car.

He looked at the map again.

THE NO TRESPASSING sign was large, the letters crude, but the meaning clear enough. Austin looked from it to Gillian.

The climb up the steep mountain reminded him of the

difference in altitude between Montana and Texas. Add to that a sleepless night in the motel knowing Gillian was just yards away and he found himself out of breath from the climb.

They'd wound up a trail of sorts from the creek bottom through boulders and brush to reach this dark hole in the cliff. It looked like rattlesnake country to him. He was glad it was winter and cold even though there were only patches of snow in the shade—just as there had been near her family's cabin.

It amazed him how different the weather could be within the state. "It's the mountains," Gillian had said when he'd mentioned it. "Always more snow near the higher mountains."

"This isn't a mountain?" he'd asked with a laugh as he looked out into the distance. He could see the lake, the frozen surface glinting in the winter sunlight.

"Have these caves always been posted like this?" he asked as he looked again at the sign.

"It's always been closed to the public," she said with a shrug.

Great, he thought. They would probably end up in jail. But if they found the ledger, they would at least have a bargaining chip to get out.

"Would your sister really come up here alone?" he asked. He couldn't help being skeptical. Rebecca was desperate, and desperate people often did extraordinary things. Still... "What about her son? She couldn't have brought him."

"It definitely isn't like Becky, I'll admit. She must have trusted someone with Andy, someone none of us knew about. The more I'm learning about my sister, the more secrets I realize she kept from me."

They were wasting time, but he wasn't that anxious

about going into the caves. He didn't think Gillian was either, now that they were here. The adorable young Luke Snider wasn't in there with his friends to entice her.

They'd stopped at an outdoor shop on the way and bought rope and headlamps, along with a first aid kit, hiking boots and a backpack. He'd brought water and a few energy bars. He hoped they wouldn't need anything else.

"I'm assuming you remember the way?" he asked.

Gillian nodded but not with as much enthusiasm as he would have liked. "It's been a while."

"Your sister remembered," he reminded her.

"Yes, that's assuming I'm right about her message. Also, this was probably the most traumatic thing that happened to my sister until she married Marc Stewart."

"You're not reassuring me," Austin said as he stepped into the cool shade of the overhanging rock. The cave opening was large. They climbed over several large boulders at the entrance before the cave narrowed and grew dark. They turned on their lamps. A few candy wrappers, water bottles and soda cans were littered on the path back into the cave. Apparently he and Gillian weren't the only ones who'd ignored the no trespassing sign.

They hadn't gone far before the cave narrowed even more. Gillian sat down on a rock that had been worn smooth and slithered through the hole feetfirst. He followed to find the cave opened up a little more once they were inside.

Austin could feel them going deeper into the mountain. They hadn't gone far when they came to a room of sorts. Water dripped from the rocks over their heads. The air suddenly felt much colder.

"You doing all right?" he asked, his voice echoing a little.

"It was easier when I was sixteen," she said, but gave him a smile.

"That was because you were in love and chasing some cute boy."

Their gazes met for a moment and he felt as he had last night after he'd kissed her. He tamped down the feeling, not about to explore it right now. Probably never. "We should keep moving."

She nodded and led the way through a slit in the rocks that curved back into a tunnel of sorts. They climbed deeper and deeper into the mountain.

MARC STEWART HAD shared one shameful secret with his wife. He was claustrophobic. He hated being in tight spaces. When he was a kid, a neighbor boy had locked him in a large trunk. He'd thought his heart was going to beat its way out of his chest before the idiot kid let him out.

As he parked next to the white SUV below the mountain, he'd told himself if he hadn't already been in a foul mood, this would have definitely put him in one. Even when he'd seen the gulch on the map, he hadn't wanted to believe it.

But at the back of his mind, he remembered bits and pieces of stories he'd overheard between his wife and her sister. Being trapped in some cave had been one of the worst experiences of Rebecca's life. Somehow her sister Gillian was to blame.

That he knew about the caves was no mystery. He'd grown up in Helena. Every kid knew about them. Most kids had explored them. Marc Stewart was the exception.

The last thing he didn't want to believe was that his wife had gone back into the cave where she'd experienced the "then" worst thing in her life. He could imagine she'd experienced worse things since then, him being one of them.

The moment he'd seen the rig the deputy had been driving parked next to the creek below the caves, he'd sworn, hating that his hunch had been right. As he cut the engine on the old pickup, he told himself that he didn't have to go *in* the caves. He could just sit right here and wait for them to come out with the ledger.

That made him feel a little better before he realized that once they saw another vehicle, even a strange one, parked down here, they might hide the ledger. Add to that, the cowboy was a sheriff's deputy. He would probably be armed.

No, Marc realized he was going to have to go up there. He wouldn't have to go inside, though. He could wait and ambush them when they came out.

Getting out, he locked the pickup and looked around. He didn't think he'd been followed, but he couldn't be sure. Not that it mattered. He should have the ledger in his possession within the hour.

Then what?

Turn it over to Victor? Make a deal with the feds? Or make a run with it?

He didn't kid himself. He would be damned lucky to get out of this alive.

He thought of Rebecca and felt his stomach churn as he climbed the mountain. The steepness of the slope forced him to stop a half dozen times on the way up. He was trying to hurry, but he couldn't seem to catch his breath. If he didn't get to the top before they came out...

What difference would it make if some Texas deputy shot him? Really, in the grand scheme of things, wouldn't that be better than what Victor probably had planned for him? he thought as he stopped to rest a dozen yards from the cave opening. Maybe that would be the kindest ending to all of this.

The thought spurred him on. He reached the opening and slipped behind a rock to wait. The winter sun was bright but not warm. He'd never been good at waiting. His mind mulled over his predicament until his head ached.

He glanced toward the opening. Still no sound. He couldn't wait any longer. He was going to have to go in. Why hadn't he realized the cave was the perfect place to dispose of the bodies? The last thing he wanted to do was kill them outside the cave where the deed would be discovered much quicker. But if he killed them in the cave, hell, maybe he could make it look like an accident. Drop some rocks on them or something.

Warmed by that idea, he pulled his gun and headed into the cave.

DEEP IN THE CAVE, Gillian stopped to get her bearings. Her headlamp flashed across the cold, dark rock. "It's just a little farther," she said. "I remember it being…easier, though, at sixteen."

"Everything is easier when you're sixteen and think you're in love."

She smiled at that. "Was there a girl when you were sixteen?"

"Nope. I was still into snakes, frogs and fishin'. It took me another year or two before I would give up a day fishing to chase a girl."

Gillian chuckled as they moved on, climbing and slipping over rocks, as they went deeper and deeper into the mountain. She thought of Becky and how she'd forced her to come along that day—on her birthday. A wave of guilt nearly swamped her when she thought of how scared Becky had been.

Then she was reminded that if she was right, Becky had come in here alone. Gillian smiled to herself, proud of her sister. She'd always felt that she needed to protect her. She realized that she'd never thought of Becky as being strong. As it turned out, Becky was a lot tougher than any of them had thought.

She saw the opening around the next bend. Rebecca hadn't been stuck exactly at this point in the cave. The opening was plenty wide. It was just that the trail dropped a good four feet as you slipped through the hole. Unable to see where she was going to land, Rebecca had frozen.

Gillian remembered a high shelf in the rocks. She scrambled up the side of the cave wall to run her hand over it, positive that would be where her sister had hidden the ledger. Nothing.

No, don't tell me all of this has been for nothing.

As she started to climb down, she saw it. A worn, thick notebook with a faded leather cover, the edges of the pages as discolored and weathered as the jacket. She grabbed it and almost lost her balance.

As usual, Austin was there to keep her from falling. He caught her, lifting her down. She clutched the ledger to her chest, tears of relief brimming in her eyes. Finally, they could stop Marc.

"Are you sure that's it?" he asked.

She held it out to him. He glanced at the contents for a moment from the light of his headlamp before handing it back.

"No, you hang on to it," she said.

He smiled and stuck it inside his jacket.

She started to move past him on the trail they'd just come down when he grabbed her arm. "Shh," he whispered next to her ear.

Gillian froze as she heard someone coming.

Austin heard what sounded like a boot sole scrapping across a rock as the person stumbled. He motioned for her to turn off her headlamp as he did the same.

It pitched them both into total darkness. "You don't think…?" Gillian whispered.

That Marc had followed them? He wasn't about to underestimate the man. A whole lot was riding on this ledger. Marc had already proven how far he would go to get his hands on it. Austin hoped it was only kids coming into the cave, but he wasn't taking any chances.

He touched Gillian's hand. She flinched in surprise before he took her hand and led her back a few yards in the cave. He remembered a recessed area they'd passed. If they could wedge themselves into it… Otherwise, if they stayed where they were, they would be sitting ducks.

He found the opening by brushing his free hand along the rocks. Stopping, he drew her closer and whispered, "There's a gap in the rocks where we can hide. Can you slip in there?" He led her to it, still holding her hand. As she slipped in, he moved back into the crevice with her, trying to make as little noise as possible. From there, with luck, they would be able to see who passed without being noticed—if they stayed quiet. If it was Marc, then he would have recognized Austin's rental SUV. If it was kids…or cops…

The footfalls on the rocks grew louder. Austin pulled his weapon, but kept it at his side, hidden, in case it was the authorities or kids.

It didn't sound like kids, though. It sounded like a single individual moving stealthily toward them.

A beam of light flickered off the walls of the cave. Austin pressed himself against Gillian as the light splashed over the rock next to him.

MARC FELT THE cave walls closing in on him. He swung his flashlight, the beam flickering off the close confines of the walls as he moved deeper into the cavern. He was having trouble breathing.

His chest hurt, his breathing a wheeze. He stumbled again and almost fell. When he caught himself on the rock wall, he lost his grip on the flashlight. It hit, rolled, smacked a rock and went out. For a few terrifying moments, he was plunged into blackness before it flickered back on.

He lurched to the flashlight, the beam dimmer than before. Picking it up, he stood, listening. Earlier when he'd entered the cave, he'd thought he heard noises. Now he heard nothing. Was it possible he'd taken the wrong turn? The thought made his heart pound so hard it hurt. He tried to settle down. There hadn't been a fork or even a tunnel through the rocks other than the one he was on large enough to move through. He couldn't have taken a wrong turn.

More to the point, Gillian and the cowboy were in here. He'd recognized the SUV. If only he could be patient enough to find them. What if they had heard him coming? What if it was a trap and the cowboy was waiting for him around the next corner of the cave?

He shone the light into the dark hole ahead of him. His breath came out in rasps. Suddenly, there didn't seem to be enough air. If he didn't get out of here now...

He spun around, banged his head on a low-hanging ledge of rock and almost blacked out as he tried not to run back the way he'd come. To hell with the ledger. To hell with Gillian and her cowboy. To hell with all of it. He was getting out of here.

Chapter Twenty-Three

Victor believed in playing the odds. He'd always known the day could come when this life he'd built might come falling down around him. He would have been a fool not to have made arrangements for that possibility. He was no fool. He had a jet at the airport and money put away in numerous accounts around the world, as well as passports in various names.

So what was he waiting for?

He looked around his mountain home. He'd grown fond of this house and Montana. He didn't want to leave. But there was a world out there and really little keeping him here.

So why wasn't he already gone? He didn't really believe that Marc was going to save the day, did he? Isn't that why he'd gone to Rebecca Stewart's hospital room himself? It had been foolish, but he'd hoped to get the information from her and then take care of the problem. That's what he did, take care of problems. He'd especially wanted to take care of her.

He hated that he'd made this personal. He'd always said it was just business. But a few times it had felt personal enough that he'd taken things into his own hands. Killing came easy to him when it was someone he felt had wronged him. In those instances, he'd liked to do it himself.

But he'd failed and he was stupid enough to try to kill her again.

Victor glanced at the clock on the wall. Was he going to wait until the FBI SWAT team arrived? Or was he going to get out while he could?

He pulled out his phone. "Take care of Marc."

Jumbo made a sound as if he'd been eagerly awaiting this particular order. "One thing you probably want to know, though—he's gone into a cave apparently looking for his missing ledger."

"A cave?"

"He's not alone. There's a white SUV here." He read off the plate number. It was the same one Victor's informant had given him.

"The Texas deputy and Marc's sister-in-law." Victor swore. "Where is this cave?"

Jumbo described the isolated gulch.

"Make sure none of them come out of the cave."

"What about the ledger?"

Victor considered. "If he has it on him, get it. Otherwise…"

AUSTIN HELD HIS BREATH. The footfalls had been close. He'd almost taken advantage of the few moments when the person had dropped his flashlight. But he hadn't wanted to chance it, not with Gillian deep in this cave with him.

What surprised him was when the footfalls suddenly retreated. The person sounded as if he were trying to run. What the—

"What happened?" Gillian whispered.

"I don't know." He kept listening, telling himself it

could be a trick. Why would the person turn back like that? The only occasional sound he heard was some distance away and growing dimmer by the minute.

"I think he left," he whispered. "Stay here and let me take a look."

He eased out of the crevice a little, his weapon ready. In the blackness of the cave, he felt weightless. That kind of darkness got to a person quickly. He listened, thought he heard retreating footfalls, and turned on his light for a split second. He'd half expected to hear the explosion of a gunshot, but to his surprise, he heard nothing. He turned his light back on and shone it the way they'd come. Whoever it had been had turned around and gone back.

The cave, as far as he could see, was empty.

He had no idea who it might have been.

Austin felt Gillian squeeze his arm a moment before she whispered, "Are they gone?"

"It appears so, but stay behind me," he whispered.

She turned on her headlamp and they headed back the way they'd come.

"YOU THINK SOMEONE will be able to make sense of this?" Gillian asked as she watched Austin thumb through the ledger. They'd stopped to catch their breaths and make sure they were still alone.

"Yeah, I do." He looked up at her. "This is big, much bigger than some guy who owns an auto shop."

She heard the worry in his voice. "If you're going to tell me that there are people who would kill to keep this book from surfacing—"

He smiled at her attempt at humor, but quickly sobered. "I'm afraid the people your brother-in-law associated with would make him look like a choirboy."

"So we need to get this to the authorities as quickly as

possible," she said and looked down toward the way out of the cave. "You think that was Marc earlier?"

"Maybe. Or one of his associates."

"Why did he turn around and go back?" she asked with new concern.

"Good question." He tucked the ledger back into his jacket. "When we get to the opening, if anything happens, you hightail it back into the cave and hide."

"You think he's waiting for us outside?"

"That's what I would do," Austin said.

"That day with my sister? I never did see Luke. I saw him go into the cave, but I never saw them come out. There must be another way out of the caves. But I have no idea where."

Austin seemed to take in the information. "Let's hope we don't need it."

Gillian followed him as they wound their way back the route they had come. The cave seemed colder now and definitely darker. She turned off her headlamp at Austin's suggestion to save on the battery, should they need it. She could see well enough with him ahead of her lighting the way.

But just the fact that he thought they might need that extra headlamp made it clear that he didn't think they would get out of here without trouble.

As MARC STUMBLED headlong out of the cave, he gulped air frantically. His whole body was shaking and instantly chilled as the December air swept across his sweat-soaked skin. He bent over, hands on his thighs, and tried to catch his breath. So intent on catching his breath, he didn't even notice Jumbo at first.

When Jumbo cleared his voice, he looked up with a

start to see the big man resting against a large boulder just outside the cave.

"Where is the ledger?" Jumbo asked.

"Inside the cave."

Jumbo lifted a heavy brow. "Why don't you have it? You were just in there."

Marc shook his head as he straightened. His gun bit into his back where he'd stuffed it in the waistband of his jeans. "My wife's sister has it." Jumbo's expression didn't change. "If you are so anxious to have it, then go into the cave and get it yourself."

Jumbo acted as if he was considering that. At the same time the thought dawned on Marc, Jumbo voiced it. "If I go in for the ledger, then what do I need you for?"

Marc's mind spun in circles. Why hadn't Jumbo just come into the cave? Something told him the big man didn't like caves any better than he did. "Good point. I guess I'd better go get it."

Jumbo smiled and stood. "Or I can simply wait until she comes out of the cave and take it from her."

Marc shook his head. "You don't want to kill her and the deputy out here where their bodies will be found too soon. Anyway, the cowboy's armed and expecting trouble. Give me a minute and I'll go back in so I can take care of them."

Jumbo's smile broadened. "You're smarter than Victor thinks you are."

He wasn't sure that was a compliment, but he didn't take the time to consider the big man's meaning. He drew his gun and fired.

AUSTIN HEARD THE gunfire outside the cave. It sounded like fireworks in the distance, but he knew it wasn't that.

"Stay here," he said to Gillian. "I'll come back for you."

She grabbed his jacket sleeve. He turned toward her, pushing back his headlamp so as not to blind her. In the ambient light, her face was etched in worry.

He drew her to him. She was trembling. "You'll be all right. I'll make sure of that."

"I'm not worried about me."

He leaned back a little to meet her eyes. "Trust me?"

She nodded. "With my life."

"I will be back." He kissed her, holding her as if he never wanted to let her go. Then he quickly broke it off. "Here." He leaned down and pulled a small pistol from his ankle holster. "All you have to do is point and shoot. Just make sure it isn't me you're shooting at."

She smiled at that. "I've shot a gun before."

"Good." He didn't want to leave her, but he hadn't heard any more shots. He had to get to the cave entrance now. "Gillian—"

"I know. Just come back."

He turned and rushed as fast as he could through the corkscrew tunnel of the cave until he could see daylight ahead. Slowing, he listened for any sound outside and heard nothing but his own breathing and the scrape of his footfalls inside the cave.

Finally, when he was almost to the cave entrance, he stopped. No sound came from outside. A trap? It was definitely a possibility. He eased his way toward the growing daylight of the world outside as he heard the roar of a vehicle engine.

He rushed forward, almost tripping over a body. The man was large. Austin didn't recognize him. It appeared he'd been shot numerous times.

Below him on the mountain, an old pickup took off in a cloud of dust and gravel. He spun around at a sound behind him to find Gillian standing in the mouth of the cave. She had the gun he'd given her in her hand.

"I thought you might need me," she said as she lowered the gun.

"Marc's not done," Gillian said as she watched Austin try to get cell phone coverage to call the police. She realized she still had the gun he'd given her. She slipped it into her pocket without thinking. Her mind was on Marc and what he would do now. "He gave up too easily. Why didn't he wait to kill us, as well?"

"He's wounded," Austin said and swore under his breath. "There is no cell phone coverage up here."

"How do you know that?"

Austin pointed to several large drops of blood a few yards from the dead man. "Right now he's headed to a doctor. Hopefully at a hospital. This is almost over."

Gillian shook her head. "I hope you're right."

He stopped trying to get bars on his phone and looked at her. "Then where is it you think he's gone?"

"If he is headed for a hospital it's my sister's. If he thinks we have the ledger and it's over… I have to get to the hospital. Now!" She could tell that Austin thought she was overreacting. "Please. I just have this bad feeling…."

"Okay. As soon as we can get cell service I'll call the hospital and make sure there is still a guard outside your sister's room and that she is safe, and then I'll call the police."

"Thank you." She couldn't tell him how relieved she was as they hurried down the mountain. Austin seemed to think that the reason Marc had left was because of his wound. The one thing she knew for sure was that Marc wasn't done.

If he'd given up on getting the ledger, then he had something else in mind. She feared that meant her sister was in danger.

VICTOR EXITED HIS car and started across the tarmac to his plane. A bright winter sun hung on the edge of the horizon, but to him it was more like a dark cloud. Jumbo hadn't gotten back to him to tell him that all his problems had been handled up the gulch. He'd been right in not waiting to see how it all sorted itself out.

He squinted and slowed his steps as he saw a figure standing next to his plane. Jumbo?

Marc Stewart stepped out of the shadow of the plane. He had his hands in the pockets of his oversize coat. "Going somewhere?"

Victor smiled, accepting that Marc wouldn't be here if Jumbo was alive. "Taking a short trip."

Marc nodded and returned his smile. "I told you I would take care of everything."

He cocked his head. "I assume you have, then."

Anger radiated off him like heat waves. "I thought you had more faith in me. Sending Jumbo to kill me? That hurts my feelings."

Victor didn't bother to answer. He'd noticed that Marc seemed to be favoring his right side. Was it possible Jumbo had wounded him?

"I can't let you get on that plane," Marc said, his hands still in his pockets. "Not without me."

"I doubt you want to go where I'm going. Nor do I suspect you're in good enough shape to travel. I'm guessing that you're wounded and that if you don't seek medical attention—"

Marc swore. "Give me the briefcase."

Victor had almost forgotten he was carrying it. He

glanced down at the metal case in his right hand. "There's nothing in there but documents. You've forced me to buy myself the same kind of protection you would have had if you'd been able to get your ledger back."

"Jumbo said I'm smarter than you think I am. Actually that was the last thing he said. Now give me the briefcase. I know it's full of money."

Before Victor could say, "Over my dead body," Marc pulled the gun from his pocket.

He glanced toward the cockpit but saw no one. Nor was there any chance of anyone appearing to turn things around. Realizing it *would* be over his dead body, Victor relented. Marc might have killed his pilot, but Victor was more than capable of flying his own plane. A flight plan had already been filed.

All he had to do was settle up with Marc. It was just money and as they say, he couldn't take it with him if Marc pulled that trigger.

Stepping toward him, Victor said, "It's all yours. A couple million in large untraceable bills." He started to hold the case out to him. At the last minute, as if his arm had a mind of its own, he swung the heavy metal case. It was just money, true enough, but it was *his* money.

He'd never thought Marc particularly fast on his feet. Nor had he thought Marc had the killer instinct. But circumstances could change a man. In retrospect he should have considered that somehow Marc had bested Jumbo. He should have considered a lot of things.

The first bullet tore through his left shoulder just above his heart. The impact made him flinch and stagger. As the second bullet punctured his chest at heart level, Marc wrenched the briefcase out of his hand.

Victor dropped to his knees and looked up at the man as his life's blood spilled out on the small airstrip's tarmac.

"I made you," he said. "You were nothing before I took you under my wing."

"Yes, you made me into the man I am now." Marc Stewart stepped to him, placed the barrel of the gun against his forehead. "You shouldn't have told Jumbo to kill me." He pulled the trigger.

Chapter Twenty-Four

Marc stood over the dead man. He wiped sweat out of his eyes, chilled to the skin and at the same time sweating profusely from the pain and the adrenaline rush.

It made him angry that Victor had put him in this position. None of this should have happened. If Rebecca hadn't— He stopped himself before he let his thoughts take him down that old road again.

What was done was done. Jumbo was dead and so was Victor. He stared down into that boy-next-door face. Victor looked good, even dead. The man's words still hung in the air. Yes, Victor had made him. He'd turned him into a killer.

Marc had been happy enough running his own body shop. Hell, he'd been proud of himself. He'd made a decent living. He hadn't needed Victor coming into his life.

But there was no going back now. *That* Marc Stewart was dead. He was now a man *he* didn't even recognize. But he felt stronger, more confident, more in control than he ever had before. Rebecca hadn't understood his frustration, his feelings of inadequacy. He'd struck out because he hadn't felt in control.

But now…he knew who he was and what he was capable of doing. He hefted the briefcase as he walked to his pickup filled with a sense of freedom. He had more money than he could spend in a lifetime. He could just take off like Victor was planning to do. He wouldn't be flying off in a jet, but he could disappear if he wanted to.

Without his son.

That thought dug in like the bullet from Jumbo's weapon that had torn through his side.

Or he could finish what he started. He thought of Rebecca. It galled him that she might win. He thought of his son. *My son,* he said under his breath with a growl.

Then there was Gillian and the cowboy deputy. He tucked the gun back into his jacket pocket as he climbed into his truck and started the engine. Once he got bandaged up… Well, the people who had tried to bring him down had no idea who they were dealing with now.

AUSTIN PUT IN the call as soon as they neared Townsend and he was able to get cell phone coverage. As he hung up, he looked over at Gillian. "The guard is outside your sister's room. Rebecca is fine. I told the doctor we are on our way."

She nodded, but he could tell she was no less worried.

He called the police, knowing there would be hell to pay for leaving the scene. Right now his main concern was Gillian, though. He'd always followed his instincts so how could he deny hers?

The drive to Bozeman took just over an hour since he was pushing it. Gillian said little on the trip. He could see how worried she was.

When his cell phone rang, he saw it was Marshal Hud Savage, his cousin-in-law. Had Hud already heard about what had happened back up the gulch?

"I was worried about you," Hud said.

With good reason, Austin thought. "I'm fine. Gillian Cooper is with me. We have Marc Stewart's ledger. We're pulling into the hospital now so Gillian can see her sister. Rebecca has regained consciousness, the doctor said. Gillian's worried that Marc is also headed there and not for medical attention. He's wounded after killing a man neither of us recognized. I spoke with the nurse earlier and all was fine, but—"

"I'll meet you there," Hud said and hung up.

THE FIRST THING Gillian saw as they started down the hallway toward Rebecca's room was the empty chair outside her door where the guard should have been. Austin had seen it first. He took off at a sprint. She wasn't far behind him, running down the hallway toward her sister's room.

Out of the corner of her eye, she saw that there was no nurse at the nurses' station. In fact, she didn't see anyone in the hallway.

The hospital felt too quiet. Her heart dropped at the thought that they'd arrived too late.

Austin crashed through the door into the room, weapon drawn, yelling, "Call security!" to her. But it was too late for that. She'd been right behind him and was now standing next to him in the center of Rebecca's room. Even if she had called security, it would have been too late.

"I wouldn't do that if I were you," Marc Stewart said. He stood shielded by Rebecca, his gun to her temple. The security guard who'd been posted at the door lay on the floor next to a nurse. Neither was moving. "Drop your gun or I will kill her and everyone else I can in this hospital."

Austin didn't hesitate, telling Gillian that he'd realized the same thing she had. Marc Stewart was no longer just an abusive bastard. He'd become a killer.

"Now kick it to me." After Austin did as he was told,

Marc turned his attention to her. "Now, you. Lock the door."

Gillian stepped to the door and locked it before turning back to the scene unfolding before her. Rebecca was conscious, her condition obviously improved, but she still looked weak. What she didn't look was scared.

"You found the ledger in the cave, didn't you?" Marc said, although he didn't sound all that interested anymore.

"I have it right here," Austin said and started to reach inside his coat.

"I wouldn't do that if I were you," Marc warned.

She could hear voices on the other side of the door. But if she turned to unlock the door, she feared Marc would shoot her sister.

"You can have it," Austin said and took a step toward Marc. "You can make a deal with it."

Marc shook his head and motioned for him to stay back. "Too late for that. Could have saved a lot of bloodshed if I had gotten the ledger back when I asked for it." Her sister made a pained sound as Marc tightened his hold on her for emphasis. "Now a lot of people are going to die because of it. Starting with you, cowboy!" He turned the gun an instant before the shot boomed.

Gillian screamed as Austin went down. She dropped to the floor next to him. She felt something heavy in her jacket pocket thud against her side. The gun. She'd forgotten about it. She reached for Austin. He'd fallen on his side. She'd expected to find him in a pool of blood, but as she knelt next to him she saw none. She could hear him gasping for breath.

"Any last words for your sister, Rebecca?" Marc demanded over the sudden pounding on the hospital room door.

Rebecca was crying. She'd dropped to the floor at Marc's feet when he'd let go of her to fire on Austin.

"Come on, don't you want to tell her how sorry you are for what you did?" Marc demanded. "I'd like to hear it. But make it quick. We don't have much time left."

Seeing that Marc's attention was on his wife, Gillian started to stick her hand in her pocket for the gun. In that instant, she saw Marc's thick leather ledger lying next to Austin, a bullet lodged somewhere in the pages. Austin's hand snaked up and took the gun from her.

"Stand up, Gillian," Marc ordered. "Rebecca, I want you to see this." He reached down to take a handful of his wife's hair and pulled her to her feet. As he did, Rebecca grabbed Austin's weapon up from the floor where he'd kicked it. She pressed the barrel into Marc's belly.

Suddenly aware of the mistake he'd made, Marc swung to hit his wife. The gunshots seemed to go off simultaneously in what sounded like cannon fire in the hospital room.

Gillian saw Marc's reaction when both Austin and Rebecca fired. He took both bullets, seeming surprised and at the same time almost relieved, she thought. Before he hit the floor, she thought she saw him smile. But he could have been grimacing with pain. It was something she didn't intend to think about as Austin got to his feet and she rushed to her sister.

In that instant, the door to the hospital room banged open as it was broken down. Marshal Hud Savage burst into the room, gun drawn. Within minutes the room was filled with uniformed officers of the law.

Chapter Twenty-Five

Christmas lights twinkled to the sound of holiday music and voices. Suddenly, a hush fell over the Cardwell Ranch living room. The only sound was the crackle of the fire. Dana saw the children all look toward the door. She had heard it, as well.

"Are those sleigh bells?" she asked in a surprised whisper.

The Cardwell brothers all exchanged a look.

Dana glanced over at Hud. "Did you—?"

"Not my doing," he said, but Dana was suspicious. She knew her husband was keeping something from all of them.

She felt a shiver of concern as she heard the sound of heavy boots on the wooden porch. A moment later, the front door flew open, bringing with it a gust of icy air and the smell of winter pine.

A man she'd never seen before stomped his boots just outside the doorway before stepping in. Because he looked so much like his brothers, though, she knew he had to be Austin Cardwell.

He carried a huge sack that appeared to be filled with presents. The children began to scream, all running to him.

"I told you Austin would be here for Christmas," she

said as she got to her feet with more relief than she wanted to admit. "I'm your cousin Dana," she said. "Come on in."

It was then that she saw the woman with Austin. She was dark haired and pretty. Dana thought she recognized her as the jeweler who lived up the road, although they'd never officially met.

She knew at once, though, that this was the woman Austin had met in the middle of the highway and the reason he'd been missing the past few days.

"This is Gillian Cooper," Austin said as he set down the large bag and put an arm around the woman.

Dana knew love when she saw it. There was intimacy between the two as well as something electric. She smiled to herself. "Come on in where it's warm. We have plenty of hot apple cider."

She ushered them into the large old farmhouse and then stood hugging herself as she looked around the room at her wonderful extended family. Having lost her family for a while years ago, she couldn't bear not having them around her now.

Her sister Stacy took their coats as Austin's brothers pulled up more chairs for them to sit in.

The children were huddled around the large bag with the presents spilling out of it.

Mugs of hot cider were poured, Christmas cookies eaten. An excited bunch of children was ushered to bed though Dana doubted any of them would be able to sleep.

"They think you're Santa Claus," she told Austin.

"Not hardly," he said.

"I'm amazed that you remembered it was Christmas," Tag teased him. "At least you didn't miss the grand opening."

"Wouldn't have missed it for the world," Austin said and they all laughed.

"Gillian," Laramie said. "Please stay safe until after New Year's. We want all five brothers together."

Austin looked over at Gillian. They'd just busted a huge drug ring. Arrests were still being made from the names in Marc's book. Rebecca and her son were finally safe. It was over, and yet something else was just beginning.

"We'll be there."

SNOW HAD BEGUN to fall as Gillian left the ranch house later that Christmas Eve night with Austin. They walked through the falling snow a short way up to a cabin on the mountainside. Austin had talked her into staying, saying it was late and Dana had a big early breakfast planned.

"It should just be you and your family," Gillian had protested.

But Dana had refused to hear it. "Do you have other plans?" Before Gillian could answer, Austin's cousin had said, "I didn't think so. Great. Austin is staying in a cabin on the hill. There is one right next to it you can stay in."

Gillian had looked into the woman's eyes and known she was playing matchmaker and this wasn't the first time. Three of Austin's brothers had come to Montana and were now either married or headed that way. She suspected Dana Cardwell Savage had had a hand in it.

Gillian was touched by Dana's matchmaking, not that it was needed. Fate had thrown her and Austin together. In a few days, they had lived what felt like a lifetime together. But they lived in different worlds, and while maybe Austin's other brothers could leave their beloved Texas, Austin was a true Texan with a job that was his life.

"Did you have fun?" Austin asked, interrupting her

thoughts as they walked toward the cabins up on the mountainside.

"I can't remember the last time I had that much fun," Gillian answered honestly.

He smiled over at her as he took her hand. "I'm glad you like my family."

"They're amazing. I don't know what makes you think you're the black sheep. Clearly, they all adore you. I think several of them are jealous of your exciting life."

Austin laughed. "They were just being polite in front of you. That's why I begged you to come with me. They couldn't be mad at me on Christmas Eve—not with you here."

"Is that why you wanted me here?"

He put his arm around her. "You know why I wanted you with me. Making my brothers behave in front of you was just icing on the cake. You're okay staying here?"

"Your cousin does know I won't be staying in that cabin by myself, doesn't she?"

"Of course. I saw the look in her eyes. She knows how I feel about you."

"She does, does she?" Gillian felt her heart beat a little faster.

Austin stopped walking. Snow fell around them in a cold white curtain. "I'm crazy about you."

"You're crazy, that much I know."

He pulled off his gloves and cupped her face in his hands. His gaze locked with hers. "I love you, Gillian."

"We have only known each other—"

He kissed her, cutting off the rest of her words. When the kiss ended, he drew back to look at her. "Tell me you don't know me."

She knew him, probably better than he knew himself. "I know you," she whispered and he pulled her close as they climbed the rest of the way to his cabin. To neither of their surprise, a fire had been lit in the stone fireplace. There was a bottle of wine and some more Christmas cookies on the hearth nearby.

"It looks as if your cousin has thought of everything," Gillian said, feeling an ache at heart level. She was falling in love with his family. She'd already fallen for Austin. Both, she knew, would end up breaking her heart when Austin returned to Texas.

She should never have let him talk her into coming here tonight. Hadn't she known it would only make things harder when the two of them went their separate ways?

She looked around the wonderfully cozy cabin, before settling her gaze on Austin. It was Christmas Eve. She couldn't spoil this night for either of them. He'd promised to stay until the grand opening of the restaurant. In the meantime, she would enjoy this. She would pretend that Austin was her Christmas present, one she could keep forever. Not one that would have to be returned once the magic of the season was over.

Because naked in Austin's arms in front of the roaring fire, it *was* pure magic. In his touch, his gaze, his softly spoken words, she felt the depth of his love and returned it with both body and heart.

THE NIGHT OF the grand opening, Austin was surprised by the sense of pride he felt as Laramie turned on the sign in front of the first Texas Boys Barbecue restaurant in Montana.

He felt a lump form in his throat as the doors were opened and people began to stream in. The welcoming crowd was huge. A lot of that he knew was Dana's doing. She was a one-woman promotion team.

"This barbecue is amazing," Gillian said as Austin

oined her and her sister and nephew. He ruffled the boy's thick dark hair and met Gillian's gaze across the table. Andy had made it through the holidays unscathed.

As soon as Rebecca was strong enough, the Bakers had brought him down to Big Sky, where the two were staying with Gillian. Rebecca had healed. Just being around her son and sister had made her get well faster, he thought. Marc was dead and gone. That had to give her a sense of peace—maybe more so because she'd had a hand in seeing that he never hurt anyone again. She was one strong woman—not unlike her sister.

"Everything is delicious," Rebecca agreed. "And what a great turnout."

Austin looked around the room, but his gaze quickly came back to Gillian. He felt her sister watching him and was sure Rebecca knew how he felt. He was in love. It still bowled him over since he'd never felt like this before. It made him want to laugh, probably because he'd given his brothers Hayes, Jackson and Tag such a hard time for going to Montana and falling in love with not only a woman but the state. He had wondered what had happened to those Texas boys.

Now he knew.

DANA THREW A New Year's party at the ranch for family and friends. Austin got to meet them all, including his cousin Jordan and his wife, Liza, Stacy's daughter, Ella, as well as cousin Clay, who'd flown up from California. The house was filled with kids and their laughter. His nephew Ford was in seventh heaven and had become quite the horseman, along with his new sister, Natalie.

As Austin looked at all of them, he felt a warmth inside him that had nothing to do with the holidays. He'd spent way too many holidays away from his family, h realized. What had changed?

He looked over to where Gillian was visiting with Stacy. Love had changed him—something he would never admit to his brothers. He would never be able to live it down if he did.

Suddenly, Dana announced that it was almost midnight. Everyone began the countdown. Ten. Nine. Eight. Austin worked his way to Gillian. Seven. Six. Five. She smiled up at him as he pulled her close. Four. Three. Two. One.

Glitter shot into the air as noisemakers shrieked. Wrapping his arms around her, he looked at the woman he was about to promise his heart to. Just the thought should have made his boots head for the door.

Instead, he kissed her. "Marry me," he whispered against her lips.

Gillian drew back, tears filled her eyes.

"I'm in love with you."

She shook her head. "I've heard all the stories your brothers tell about you. *All Austin needs is a woman in distress and it's the last we see of him.* Austin, you've spent your life rescuing people, especially women. I'm just one in a long list. I bet you fell in love with all of them."

"You're wrong about that," he said as he cupped her face in his hands. "And don't listen to my brothers," he said with a laugh. "You can't believe anything they tell you, especially about me."

"I suspect your brothers are just as bad as you. After listening to how they met their wives, I'd say saving damsels in distress runs in this family."

He grinned. "You're the one who saved me."

Her eyes filled with tears.

"Remember our first kiss?" he asked.

"Of course I do."

"I knew right then you were the one. Come on, you felt it, didn't you?"

Gillian hated to admit it. "I felt...*something.*"

He laughed as he drew her closer and dropped his mouth to hers for another slow, tantalizing kiss. It would have been so easy to lose herself in his kiss.

She pushed him back. True, the holidays had been wonderful beyond imagination. She'd fallen more deeply in love with Austin. But her life was here in Big Sky, especially since she couldn't leave her sister and Andy. Not now.

She said as much to him, adding, "You love being a sheriff's deputy and you know it."

He dragged off his Stetson and raked a hand through his thick dark hair. Those dark eyes grew black with emotion. "I did love it. It was my life. Then I fell in love with you."

She shook her head. "What about the next woman in distress? You'll jump on your white horse and—"

"Laramie needs someone to keep an eye on the restaurant up here. I've volunteered."

She stared at him in shock. "You wouldn't last a week. You'd miss being where the action is. I can't let you—"

"I've been where the action is. For so long, it was all I've had. Then I met you. I'm through with risking my life. I have something more important to do now." He dropped to one knee. "Marry me and have my children."

"*Our* children," she said.

"I'm thinking four, but if you want more..."

She looked into his handsome face. "You're serious?"

"Dead serious. You may not know this, but I was the driving force originally behind my brothers and I open-

ing the first barbecue joint. I can oversee the restaurant—
and take care of you and kids and maybe a small ranch
with horses and pigs and chickens—"

Just then, they both realized that the huge room had
grown deathly quiet. As they turned, they saw that everyone was watching.

Austin shook his head at his brothers not even caring
about the ribbing he would get. He turned his attention
back to Gillian. "Say you'll marry me or my brothers
will never let me live this down," he joked, then turned
serious. "I don't want to spend another day without you.
Even if it isn't your life's dream to become a Cardwell—"

"I can't wait to be a Cardwell," she said and pulled
him to his feet. "Yes!" she cried, throwing herself into
his arms. He kissed her as the crowd burst into applause.

From in the crowd, Dana Cardwell Savage looked
to where her cousin Laramie was standing. "One more
cousin to go," she said under her breath and then smiled
to herself.

* * * * *

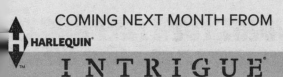

"The woman in Greenleaf Bar was you?"

"You don't remember?"

"Vaguely."

He struggled to put things in perspective. That had been
a hell of a night. He'd stopped at the first bar he'd come
to after leaving the rodeo. A blonde had sat down next to
him. As best he remembered, he'd given her an earful about
the rodeo, life and death as he'd become more and more
inebriated.

She must have offered him a ride back to his hotel since
his truck had still been at the bar when he'd gone looking
for it the next morning. If Brit was telling the truth, the
woman must have gone into the motel with him and they'd
ended up doing the deed.

If so, he'd been a total jerk. She'd been as drunk as him
and driven or she'd willingly taken a huge risk.

Hard to imagine the woman staring at him now ever

being that careless or impulsive.

"Is that your normal pattern, Mr. Dalton?" Brit asked "Use a woman to satisfy your physical needs and then rid off to the next rodeo?"

"That's a little like the armadillo calling the squirre roadkill, isn't it? I'm sure I didn't coerce you into my bed i I was so drunk I can't remember the experience."

"I can assure you that you're nowhere near tha irresistible. I have never been in your bed."

"Whew. That's a relief. I'd have probably died o frostbite."

"This isn't a joking matter."

"I'm well aware. But I'm not the enemy here, so you car quit talking to me like I just climbed out from under a slimy rock. If you're not Kimmie's mother, who is?"

"My twin sister, Sylvie Hamm."

Twin sisters. That explained Brit's attitude. Probably considered her sister a victim of the drunken sex urges he didn't remember. It also explained why Brit Garner looked familiar.

"So why is it I'm not having this conversation with Sylvie?"

"She's dead."

Find out what happens next in
MIDNIGHT RIDER
by Joanna Wayne,
available January 2015 wherever
Harlequin Intrigue® books and ebooks are sold.

HIEXP69806R

SPECIAL EXCERPT FROM

H HARLEQUIN
™

INTRIGUE®

Read on for an excerpt from
THE SHERIFF
The first installment in the
WEST TEXAS WATCHMEN series
by Angi Morgan

Mysterious lights, a missing woman, a life-long secret
revealed…all under a star-studded West Texas sky.
Sheriff Pete Morrison must protect a gorgeous witness,
Andrea Allen, from gun smugglers and…herself.

"We've got to get you out of here."

"I am not helpless, Pete. I've been in self-defense courses my entire life. And I know how to shoot. My gun's in the bag we left outside."

Good to know, but he wasn't letting her near that bag. He dropped the key ring on the floor near her hands. "Find one that looks like it's to a regular inside door. Like a broom closet. I'm going to lock you inside."

"Are you sure they're still out there?"

"The chopper's on the ground. The blades are still rotating. No telling how many were already here ready to ambush us." He watched two shadows cross the patio. "Let's move. Next to the snack bar, there's a maintenance door. Run. I'll lay down cover if we need it."

They ran. He could see the shadows but no one followed. Hopefully they didn't have eyes on him or Andrea. He heard the keys and a couple of curses behind him, then a door swung open enough for his charge to squeeze through.

He saw the glint of sun off a mirror outside. They were watching.

"Can you lock the door? Will it lock without the key?"

"I think so."

"Keep the keys with you. I don't need them. Less risky." Bullets could work as a key to unlock, but they might not risk injuring Andrea. He was counting on that.

"But, Pete—"

"Let me do my job, Andrea. Once you're inside, see if you can get into the crawl space. They just saw you open the door. Hide till the cavalry arrives."

"You mean the navy. He won't let us down," she said from the other side of the door. "This is his thing, after all."

Pete had done all he could do to hide her. Now he needed to protect her.

Find out what happens next in
THE SHERIFF
by Angi Morgan,
available January 2015 wherever
Harlequin Intrigue® books and ebooks are sold.